Totally Bound Publishing books by Nicole Dennis:

Southern Charm
Rules of the Chef

I0570495

Southern Charm

RULES OF THE CHEF

NICOLE DENNIS

Rules of the Chef
ISBN # 978-1-78184-772-5
©Copyright Nicole Dennis 2014
Cover Art by Posh Gosh ©Copyright March 2014
Interior text design by Claire Siemaszkiewicz
Totally Bound Publishing

RULES OF THE CHEF

Dedication

To RJ, who helped me get this series started. To all my betas who helped me make these guys better. I hope everyone enjoys these stories.

Chapter One

"I can't believe you went ahead and sold the Charm without alerting me of your final decision. I thought we were considering our options, not going ahead with a contract," Dakota Mitchell said. He couldn't keep the irritation out of his voice.

The familiar work he was engaged in helped him from losing complete control over his anger. Running his sharp chef's knife through a pile of onions, bell peppers, celery, and several cloves of garlic with skill and ease was one way of not using the blade on something or someone else. Lifting the knife, he waved it at his best friend and now apparently former partner in their business, Edward Schaffer. "What were you thinking? One more year, I told you. One more season and we would have been fine and back in the black. The entire region is recovering from the damn oil spill, but everyone is starting to come back to the Gulf."

"Lisa and I don't have any more money to put into the Charm. Either we sold or the bank was going to foreclose on the mortgage," Edward said, shoving a hand in his pocket. "Things were at the point of no return. We're too deep in the red and I saw no other way to save the Charm. I had no other choice. We couldn't wait for another season, not with the pre-season bookings."

"Shit, Ed. I would have given you what I could—"

"No, it'll be too much on my financials and personal fortitude to lift the Charm out of the mortgage debts and keep her running. I have nothing left to invest and I'm close to losing my home. I know as well as you do what you have in the bank. You don't have that kind of capital. The one thing holding the Charm is your restaurant and I don't want you to lose it to foreclosure."

"You didn't give me the chance to help. I could have signed a new loan or some kind of modification." Dakota couldn't stop the disappointment coloring his voice.

"It's too late to argue now. I did what was best for my family, for my health, and for the Charm. It was a difficult decision, but one I had to make. I'm sorry but papers are signed passing my share over to the buyers."

"I didn't sign over my share nor do I plan on signing over anything. This restaurant is still my piece." Dakota tugged over a bowl of washed, fresh Gulf shrimp to finish preparing it for his trademark gumbo. Needing a few moments to deal with the bombshell dropped on him he turned back and checked the color of the roux, giving it a few good stirs. In another large pot, he checked the simmering stock and his timer. He picked up the strainer and skimmed off the fat and scum from the top.

What was going to happen without Edward being the other half of the hotel? Where did the decision leave Dakota and the staff? Who had bought the restaurant? Listing the questions in his head, he turned to face his friend. Edward had suffered a mild stroke last year and it had aged him.

"I told them you were keeping your share of ownership. No one is going to ask you to sign over anything. I made sure it was in the contract. They're sending one of their fellas from management to look things over."

Dakota snorted his disbelief, he couldn't help himself. "You mean they're coming here to change things," he said harshly. "It's what they're going to do, you know. No matter what they promise, they'll take all the beauty and magic out of the Charm and make her ordinary, boring and another bland place no one will remember."

"Dakota, I'm sorry. It wasn't easy to find a buyer. Please. I wish there could be another way."

"I understand. I'll deal with things." Dakota took his flash of temper out on the large gray shrimps sitting on his bamboo covered work surface. He snapped a head, fins and legs off one crustacean. A quick slice with a small knife and he peeled off the thin shell. Another slice and he yanked out the black vein and guts from the back. He tossed all the scraps into a container to make stock from the tasty shells and guts.

Dakota saw Edward shudder out of the corner of his eye.

"Must you do that in front of me?" Edward muttered with another shiver. A grimace curled his lips and emphasized the lines in his face.

When Dakota looked closely at Edward, someone he thought of like a father, he noticed he appeared tired, exhausted, but there was a spark of something in his eyes. Relief? Jeez, all Dakota was being here was selfish. Edward had attempted to talk about selling up on so many occasions and all Dakota had done was push his words to one side with his normal 'we'll be fine'. Guilt climbed inside him and with it came his usual sense of humor to dispel the emotion.

Glancing from the small crustacean to his friend, Dakota lifted and wiggled it in Edward's face. "What? Don't want to eat the little shrimp?" He deliberately deepened and thickened his Southern accent to annoy Edward further with the teasing.

When Edward smiled, it reached his eyes this time. The teasing was familiar and somehow dangling the shrimp in Edward's face was enough to break the unsettled anger. He batted Dakota's hand away. "Knock it off, Dakota," he said with a shudder. "It has eyes."

Dakota chuckled knowing the shrimp always got a rise out of his friend. He shook his head and focused back on the matter in hand. "Who bought it anyway?" *Was that a reasonable question to ask or will it just bring up the anger again?* When Edward paused, Dakota immediately knew he wouldn't like the answer.

"The Ashford family of the Ashford Hotels chain was looking to extend south and create boutique hotels. They purchased my portion of the Charm. The chain is world renowned. People know what to expect in whatever Ashford Hotel they stay in and I hope the same holds true when they take over here."

"I don't believe you went to them. The Ashfords? Do you mean the ripping apart and standardizing everything Ashfords? You would let them tear her to bits?"

"I'm sorry. It's not like we had a queue of people wanting to invest. Dakota—"

"What am I going to do with a stinking hotel conglomerate coming down on my ass?" Temper coated every word and he concentrated on his breathing to calm himself down.

"Work the angles? You still own fifty percent."

Another snort came from Dakota as he stopped handling the shrimp, sanitized his hands, and stirred the roux. "They'll rip us apart and put us back together so badly the Charm won't be what we know anymore."

"Like I said, Dakota, I made sure fifty percent remains yours."

"It doesn't matter. The first thing on their list to change will be to own my fifty percent," Dakota said morosely. "They're gonna take away everything you and I built into the Charm and toss it out in one foul swoop. They don't care for the Gulf, the small town, or her folks. All they're interested in is another building to put their stamp on and get more money. Hell, I'm telling you now, if they don't get their money back within six months or less, they'll knock down the Charm. When they do, I'll lose everything I built. I don't know if the restaurant will survive if they close down the B&B operations. What would I do with a three-story empty building attached to my restaurant? It's kinda tacky to have it standing there, hoping someone will come along and do something strange. No, way I see it, if the Charm shuts down, so does the Delights."

Edward winced at the summary. "Kota, you can't know their plans. They seemed more than interested in what the Charm was all about."

Dakota wagged a shrimp at Edward. "I bet you a hundred bucks. Six months from now, the Charm isn't going to resemble the beautiful and graceful building we love. She's gonna end up being some boring run-of-the-mill motel and no one will come and see her or my restaurant."

"It doesn't have to be that way."

"It's not our fault people aren't coming back. It's the damn oil spill, but tourists are returning. Just need to get the word out. I mean, damn, look at these shrimp. Plump, juicy and they taste damn good. Beaches are white and pristine. Weather is gorgeous. Shops are open and need customers. Hell, all we need are more people with a few bucks in their wallets."

"Everyone needs more bucks in their wallets. It's called a recession."

"Bah!" Dakota waved a different crustacean in the air before slicing it down the back and removing its vein. "Folks out there still have money. Need to find them and bring them down."

"Lisa and I can't anymore. We're out and the new folks are in."

"Fine. Fine. I'll deal with this new interloper. Who is it? This new manager you said is coming down to check us out. Who is he? When is he coming?"

"Samuel Ashford. There wasn't an exact date. He should be here either sometime today or tomorrow," Edward offered warily.

Dakota couldn't believe what Edward told him. *Ashford?*

"An Ashford?" This was the icing on the cake. "Is this one of the family members who owns the hotels Ashford? Today or tomorrow! What the hell? You waited until the last minute to tell me what's happening so I can't fight back."

Edward nodded. "You don't give me much choice."

"Great. Probably some bigwig with a cell phone stuck to his head, a pen and pad in his hand, or a snooty 'yes, sir' assistant following his every move."

"Dakota..." Edward warned.

"What?" Dakota said, acting like he had no idea what Edward's warning meant.

"You can hold onto the fifty percent control you have. Use it to your advantage and try pouring on a little southern charm with them. I know you have manners somewhere in your hard head."

Dakota didn't call his friend of ten years on the flippant response. Edward was attempting, in his own way, to make everything seem fine. "That's the hotel's name, not my character," Dakota finally said grumpily.

"You're a Southern boy. I know you gotta have charm somewhere."

"Are you calling me a country song?" Dakota wiggled the big chef's blade at his friend. He would play the 'nothing to worry about' game if it meant that Edward stayed away from stress. Edward gave him a grateful smile.

"If the shoe fits," Edward teased. "I am sorry. You know I wouldn't have done this if there was any other way."

"I know." He stopped what he was doing and placed the knife on the chopping board. Sighing he crossed his arms over his chest. "I've known for a while Lisa has been on at you to retire. I wish you could have retired on a high with money in your pocket and a heap of good memories."

"As soon as Deepwater Horizon happened, I knew it would never be an option," Edward offered. "We used to make good money from this place, but we got the huge hit from the downfall from Hurricanes Katrina and Rita. It's not the same in the Gulf, not anymore. We could barely afford the increased insurance premiums, let alone make all the needed repairs around this place. Lisa and I have very little for retirement and need to figure how to spend the rest of our lives together with some comforts."

Dakota felt every single ounce of anger drain from his body at the simple words. His friend looked tired, beaten, and pushing back his own despair, his own anger, Dakota reached out with compassion.

"Tell Lisa I was fine with it all." Lisa and Edward had been married so long that Dakota teased them about how they photographed and filmed their marriage in black and white. Lisa would be sitting in their rooms worrying about what Edward was telling Dakota.

Edward looked grateful and sad at the same time. "If there had been any other way, Kota." He held out a hand.

Dakota eyed the hand—held out in peace—and decided that ten years of friendship meant more than a single handshake. In a characteristic move he pulled Edward in for a close hug. When had his friend got so thin? So frail? They stayed that way for a while, locked in the embrace of friendship until Edward pulled back.

"You stink of fish, Kota," he teased.

Dakota smiled. He could do this. He could act like someone hadn't pulled his entire world from underneath him and flipped him upside down. Gently, he poked his friend in the chest.

"Yep, and now, so do you."

Chapter Two

Samuel Ashford parked the car on the side of the blacktop and checked his navigation system. He wondered how it had even found this tiny town of Shore Breeze at the end of a peninsula sticking out between a deep busy bay heading toward the more popular Pensacola and the vast Gulf. According to the Charm's simple website and his own research the hotel should be the turnoff he had passed. No matter what, he didn't want to get lost on this single stretch of highway.

This was freaking typical how he was going to be late for his first meeting at the Southern Charm. Being late made him tense and he pulled at his deep red tie and the collar of his pristine white shirt. *Fuck, it is hot today.* He didn't know how anyone could expect to enjoy a break in all this heat, let alone work in it.

Still not sure where he was, he glanced down at the papers spread on his passenger seat and checked the listed address against the paperwork. Brilliant, yet again he had gotten himself lost.

'I'm not sure you're ready for this.' His dad's words echoed in his mind, and not for the first time he wondered if maybe his dad was right. Maybe twenty-four was too young to be involved in a project of this size. It didn't matter that he had been part of the family hotel chain from birth, he still felt like he had so much to learn. Conceived, born and educated in Ashford Hotels meant that the business was in his blood but still...this? This was maybe too much.

'For goodness sake, Michael, he's absolutely perfect for this job.' God, his mom thought he was invincible. Like he was able to do anything he could set his mind to. The boutique type hotels in tourist hotspots had been her idea to begin with. From day one she had intended her four children to learn the business in one of the far-flung and smaller hotels she had found. The Southern Charm was one of them. Ten bedrooms and on the coast ravaged by the oil spill in April 2010, its occupancy rates had nosedived. It appeared from Samuel's research that the only thing keeping the doors open was the restaurant, which catered for locals and visitors alike.

Various reviews spoke of gorgeous, mouth-watering food tasting fresh from the sea. The chef, Dakota Mitchell, was also Samuel's new partner.

"I don't like the fact we own fifty percent." This had been the single bit of input Samuel had brought up at the meeting with his parents. Everything he thought about the acquisition of this new hotel had been placed in the simple statement he'd made. His mother had chosen him to take charge of this project for the company.

"The co-owner hasn't needed to sell his share, but it was too good a deal to pass up buying the other half," his dad had said.

"This might be a good thing, dear." His mom always had her opinion and wasn't afraid to use it. "Trial by fire when every decision you make has to be run by this half owner. It will make your life interesting." She'd rifled through the paperwork and lifted out a ream of reviews on the Southern Charm restaurant and hotel. "And look, Sam, he's pretty."

Samuel looked down now at the same picture. The layout was typical review style with a photo of the chef and various dishes among paragraphs, which included words like 'sublime', 'characterful' and 'charming'. Yes the guy was pretty, all artfully tousled golden blond hair and startling sky blue eyes. But there was stubbornness in those eyes and the tilt of his pretty chin. Pretty? What was he like? Dakota was far from pretty. He was handsome, rugged, and Sam needed to stop using the adjective 'pretty' with men.

"Kath, for goodness sake," his dad had intervened in his wife's attempt to suggest that Sam may enjoy his new post for reasons other than working the hotel angle.

Coming out to his family had been painless enough. A few tears, a few concerns, even one huge row with his eldest brother, Simon, but nothing had occurred that was either heart-rending, family-ripping, or other worst case scenarios he'd heard others had gone through when they came out. According to his family, him being gay was cool and part of his identity, but didn't change how they felt toward him. His dad had gone further and pointed out that it might work in his favor one day. Always count on Dad to find the work angle.

Sighing inwardly and checking the clock one last time he swung back onto the road and used the next available turning point to go back the way he'd come.

The sun was mercilessly hot out here as it neared its midday zenith, Sam turned up the air con another notch. He wondered if arriving with ice on his eyelashes would keep him cool while he stamped his authority on this new place. Probably not.

Finding the road this time was easy. It was a lot clearer coming from the other way. Though, he wasn't sure if he could even call this dirt and gravel strewn path a road. "Note to self," he intoned to his phone, which recorded immediately. "Signage from main road is appalling. Road also needs work with smoothing and paving." The road down to where the Charm should be was clear of potholes but narrow and he carefully eased his Porsche as far to the right as he could just in case he met someone coming the other way. It was all nature at its best and untouched glory. Ancient oak trees and knobby cypresses stretched their limbs across one another, most covered with dangling grayish-green Spanish moss. Grass was over a foot high. "Check on landscaping for the road."

Finally he rounded the last corner and stopped short at the sight of the dilapidated stone and iron fence. A useless gate hung open. On one post was the simplest of signs —

Southern Charm
Bed & Breakfast
Established 1903
Southern Delights — Fresh Seafood Restaurant

"Are you kidding me? That's it? That's what they call a sign? No, no, no, this will not do. Not do at all." Samuel stared dumbfounded at the undecorated, plain, black-print sign. "Note to self — get a new sign by gate. Check on security around gate. Update or fix both the gate and fence." Pushing down on the gas, he drove through the gate and went around another bend. The road wrapped around a decaying stone and marble fountain before it widened into a gravel parking area. He wasn't sure about the fountain. There was no beautiful fall of water, only a tiny trickling bit from the top. Stunned at what he saw before him, he killed the engine and parked where he was.

"Oh, wow, I didn't expect this. What an old beauty."

The Southern Charm was like something out of a story book. The pictures he had in his research didn't do it justice at all. Whitewashed cedar clapboard shingles covered the exterior, the boards aged to shades of gray by the sea and air. The gravel walk-up led to a large wrap-around porch with inviting rocking chairs. A graceful Adirondack porch swing hung in one corner. There were two more upper levels connected to the various suites. None of the faded exterior took anything away the appeal of the home. The three-story home was an exquisite blend of old Florida summerhouse charm and Southern antebellum elegance. Surrounded by old moss-covered oaks and cypresses, the Charm overlooked the water.

"Note to self—we need more pictures taken."

Parking his car in the gravel lot, he climbed out of the Porsche. The heat in the air from the midday sun caused him to break into a sweat almost immediately. There was a trickle of moisture down his back and tightness around his throat where his collar and tie sat. Heat wasn't on his 'to do' list.

After walking around, he opened the trunk and stared down at the limited number of bags. He had enough to cover himself for the six weeks he intended to stay. If he needed anything else, he would ask someone to send it down. Thanks to his family's multiple trips, he had learned how to travel light and efficiently. Ingrained within him from childhood, he knew how to pack and stretch a miniscule wardrobe. His home, if he could call it that, was a room in Ashford Central Park. Not a room overlooking the park. Rooms like that were for guests—and he was never actually in his room much anyway—but it was nonetheless comfortable and home. His sister had another room down the corridor.

Juggling all his bags was not an option. He didn't want to arrive at his new place of work struggling with luggage. Choosing just to take his computer case he locked the Porsche. Best foot forward. One wouldn't create more sweat.

Adopting the persona he had decided on, a confident hotelier from a family of hoteliers, he entered through the front door and soothed by the coolness of the tiled spacious foyer. In combination with the air conditioning, two plantation bamboo-style fans swirled the cool air in a lazy fashion. Bliss after the heat outside. There was no one behind the reception desk, but a large bell sat on the side with the missive 'Ring for service' sat on a gilded card.

This wasn't a great introduction to the Charm. Someone had to be expecting his arrival. Could this be how the South handled the front desk? He'd heard things were different below the Mason–Dixie line, but this was ridiculous. He had thought it was all about warm hospitality and family down here.

He rang the bell and added a clipped "Hello?" to his announcement of arrival. Complete silence met the bell and he waited patiently. This was ridiculous.

How many guests had the Charm lost by having no one at reception?

"Sorry. Sorry. I'm here." The voice came from behind him and he turned.

Faced with a short woman of indeterminate age he extended his hand. "Samuel Ashford," he said briefly.

"Elise Jeffries, I'm the front desk and daytime manager. Welcome to Southern Charm," the lady responded. She took his hand in a surprisingly firm grip. "Apologies for lack of welcome but there's a problem in the kitchen and I got caught up in it."

"No worries," he lied. There was a problem in the kitchen. He thought the kitchen was the one thing keeping this place from sinking completely. How could there be problems? The instinct to turn tail and run hit him like a sledgehammer. This was not a good start to his inspection. "Is it something major?"

"Oh no, it's nothing major to damage anything. Dakota is the only one who can stop the smoke alarm. I set it off burning toast and he was in the shower."

"The smoke alarm is going off. Okay?"

"See, I'm five-four," she said and indicated her short self. "Dakota is six-three—" She waved above her head. "So he can reach the alarm just by lifting a hand. Last time I tried it I fell off the stool. I swear the thing hates me. Anyway, I had to get him out of the shower and he's all naked and wet and—" She stopped. There was a definite twinkle in her eye as she explained all of this.

"Uh–huh, got the mental picture." It was all he could say. Blond, blue-eyed Dakota—*who calls their kid Dakota?*—was tall. Way tall. Much taller than his own five-eleven. And Samuel, who let's face it wasn't one to get much in the way of action, had missed wet, naked, *pretty* Dakota fixing the alarm. He wondered how naked the man was. With that thought, his cock sat up and took notice. He damned the sudden awakening of his quieted libido. He didn't need a distraction from his first big job.

"Ashford... Ashford... Oh, are you the representative of the company who bought out Edward's share of the Charm?"

Samuel lifted an eyebrow. "I am."

"A special welcome to you and thank you for coming, I hope you love our beautiful place. Anyway, let me have you sign the registry and I'll get the key," she said as she pulled up a large leather-bound book and turned it for him to sign.

"Do you still use this for all your guests?"

"It helps to back up our ancient computer system."

"Why isn't the computer system working?" Samuel took the pen and scrawled out his name and information.

"Sorry, sorry, I don't want to alarm or worry you. Things do work around here, I promise, but like other items the computer is temperamental and outdated. I learned ways to work around the problems." Elise winced and covered her face for a moment. "Sorry. I'm babbling. Let me show you to your room." She leaned over the counter and snagged a key then led him up a winding flight of stairs to the left of the reception area. "We've put you in the Starfish Room. It has the best views of the ocean—"

"You shouldn't," Samuel interrupted. "We should be saving the best rooms for guests."

She looked back at him with a curious expression. His words registered and she shook her head. "Don't worry, that isn't a concern with this room. It's on the third floor and reserved for owners and staff. You'll see why."

And he did. Tacked to the door was a bronze plaque with an engraved name. Tucked up under the eaves, the room was tiny and far too small to rent out. Not much bigger than the double bed, it was a wonder they had managed to fit in both a cabinet and an adjoining bathroom. There were several paintings and knick-knacks with starfish on the walls and furniture. It had a charm about it that reminded Samuel of summers at his Gramma's house in Martha's Vineyard. The quilt had clearly been hand sewn with a starfish pattern, and the room painted a brilliant white with sand colored accents that pulled in the sun. He sighed with relief at the air conditioning. Placing his case on the cabinet he looked out of the window. Okay so it wasn't the green of Central Park but the ocean was magnificent here. Sparkling blue and green with the sun glinting off wave tips as they hit the shore, the view was picture postcard.

"It's beautiful. I haven't been to the ocean in years."

Elise moved to stand next to him at the window. "This window has seen many changes these past few years. Such hardship all of us Gulf shore residents faced."

"What kinds of changes?"

"It's part of what happened to the entire area with the historic hurricane season in 2010. We had everything from flooding, lost trees, homes wiped out and beach erosion."

"Those storms can be quite destructive." He remembered what the east coast had gone through with just one big hurricane—Sandy. He couldn't imagine what it would be like with multiple Sandys hitting the coast, every single summer.

"They were, and the damn oil spill didn't help the situation."

"You're talking about the Horizon."

"Back before the damage done by the oil derrick, things were perfect. Instead of going out for the various fishing seasons, we could see the boats carrying out the clean-up with all those special barriers dragged behind them, and catching the slick darkness from the sea. It was a terrible tragedy for us."

"I imagine." He didn't. He couldn't know what it had been like. His exposure to the oil spill had been from the safety of his room on the regular CNN reports.

"The beach was filled with sunbathers all year around. Now it's rare for it to be full any time of the year. They're starting to come back, but not in previous numbers. Edward did his best at working on the issue, but with his stroke last year, he couldn't keep up with the hours and stress."

"It's a tragedy to miss this white sand and warm water." Though he wanted to know how warm the water was, Samuel wasn't sure he could indulge during the trip. He was here on business. Business came first.

"Anyway, no one has given up on the Gulf and her beauties yet. We're a strong, stubborn group of folk. I'll let you get settled in and maybe I can show you to Dakota."

"Thank you. Am I correct in guessing he will be in the kitchen?"

"Usually. He's either there or the beach. He likes to relax there before the dinner rush."

"Don't worry yourself. I'll find him when I am ready."

There would be no planned meeting. He needed this surprise visit to see for himself what a mess this place was in.

And decide if it was worth keeping open at all.

Chapter Three

After thoroughly cursing and fidgeting with the screaming smoke alarm, Dakota got the blasted thing to shut off and reset. After tossing the battery in the trash, he washed his hands. He fixed Elise some new toast, this time perfectly browned, and set it on the plate. She would retrieve it after dealing with the new guest. He barely heard the tinny of the old bell with the shrill pitched alarm. He checked the gentle bubbling pot of gumbo, giving it another few deep stirs, and used a spoon to check the flavors. Approving with a *hmm*, he added another half palmful of salt and stirred. He hiked up the waistband of the board shorts he'd yanked on when Elise had yelled for him.

Turning, he saw Elise walking in and shook his head. "No using my kitchen," he teased in a playful tone.

Laughing, she lifted on her toes to press a kiss to his cheek. "But you know I love to catch you mid-shower. You're too yummy to watch when you're all wet and naked," she teased, reaching into the fridge for a jar of jam. Grabbing it, she searched for a knife in a drawer.

He pressed a hand to his damp chest and fluttered his lashes. "I wish I swung your way, darling. You would be the first I would come after." He reached into the right drawer and gave her the knife.

"Thanks." She spread a good helping of homemade blackberry jam on the slices and licked a droplet from her thumb. She tossed the knife into the sink and put away the jar.

"Hey, you need to be nice to my kitchen. There is a dishwasher and I'm not it," he grumbled. "I don't know if I would come after you if I liked your girly parts."

"Girly parts? My girly parts are awesome. Yeah, right, you wouldn't race after me. I don't know if I would bother to let you chase me." Snatching one of his dish towels, Elise twirled it and snapped it against his hip.

"Ow! Hey!" He rubbed his ass where the towel had snapped him. He rolled his larger bath towel and waved it at her. "I got one too now!"

"Don't you dare!" She raced around the edge of the counter to get away from his extended reach.

"Apologize to the sink for your horrid mistreatment." He twirled the towel.

Her eyes widened and she laughed. Snatching her plate of toast, she waved a hand at him. "Get on with your dreamy wet self. Put some clothes on before you scare the guests."

"Did one come in?"

"Yup and he set my gaydar off too. He's also cute as heck. I think he could be a hot one for you. You should give it a chance."

Dakota walked to the opening. "Perhaps I'll check him out. I could use a little fling. It'll work off the damn stress before this corporate bigwig shows and changes everything I love."

"You don't want to scare this one off. We need all the guests we can get." Elise was teasing but Dakota had seen the bookings to prepare the menus for breakfast. He wasn't completely clueless about how bad things were in the way of pre-bookings. He wasn't going to be scaring anyone off in the near future. His seriousness must have shown on his face as Elise stopped by the door and tilted her head. "Kota, we'll get through this."

"Yeah, but how much will remain in the end?" Dakota muttered. Elise left with a smile of encouragement. Dakota moved around the back hallway and the stairs to his private suite under the eaves. He needed to get dressed and return to his kitchen. At least he had some control in one part of his home.

I wouldn't have a home if I lose my share. Shit, I would have to figure out where to create and supply a new restaurant, a place to live, and all kinds of other crap. I don't need this pressure or stress. What a crock of horse shit! His thoughts were almost as chaotic as a smoke alarm in a quiet room. Shoving a hand through his wet hair, pushing the damp strands off his face, he used the towel to dry his hair at the back.

Climbing the stairs, he stared down at the floor while he rubbed the towel over his nape. On the top floor, Dakota went down the empty hall. He cursed in surprise when he banged into something hard. A body, it seemed, as he saw his bare feet tangled with pricey leather loafers. Feeling their combined mass go off balance, he wrapped his wet arms and towel around the other form, and twisted to take the brunt of the fall. His head rapped hard against the floor and wall after his ass hit the carpet.

"Holy hell!" There was a harsh biting ache in his hip and an answering throb in his skull.

Glancing up, his eyes a little dazed and blurry, he felt more than saw the shorter figure—a man— pressed against him. A noticeable erection ground against his lower belly and it wasn't his. It sharpened his attention through the haze of pain and caused his cock to take notice. He groaned when their erections bumped together.

Their legs tangled—it had been one hell of a long time since he'd had the heavy weight of a guy pressing him to the floor. Unable to help himself, he breathed in the delicious cologne and soapy scent of the man before he admired the honey-highlighted brunet color of his hair. The weight of a suit and tie brushed against his skin.

"Why can't you look out where you're going?" the guy said. "I was clearly on one side, not even in your path."

Dakota felt like retorting *'Well, duh, had a freaking towel over my head'*, but he didn't. Instead he offered rational defense, "I didn't expect anyone up on the staff and owners' floor. I'm the one on the bottom here. You knocked me over."

"You tangled our feet together and knocked us off balance. I had no other choice except to go down."

Dakota forced the smaller man to roll onto the thin carpet and hardwood floor. He moved his aching erection to a different side to relive some pressure. He pressed a hand against the growing knot of pain on the back of his head. "Jeez. This isn't what I need on top of everything else, a freaking bump and headache."

"Are you all right?" Guest on the Wrong Floor said.

"I whacked the living hell out of my head. How do you think I am?" Dakota grinned as he looked across at Mr Uptight. "We can only blow out so much cold air to chill people off. You should lose a few layers."

"I'm not here on vacation. This is a business visit. I'm here to oversee things and was assigned this room when I requested it. The lady at the front desk said this room wasn't for guests."

"Business? What kind of business? Florida businessmen are dressed in business casual. No tie required."

"Should I presume you're staff?"

"A little more than staff, I'm the chef and owner...co-owner of the Charm. I belong up here. Dakota Mitchell," Dakota said. "You're on the wrong floor."

The man blinked caramel brown eyes. Dakota found an intense interest in the long brown lashes that surrounded them. "Samuel Ashford. I represent the new co-owner and I belong on this floor."

"Ashford? You're Samuel Ashford? You're early, I wasn't expecting you until later."

Dakota scrambled and pushed himself well away from the gorgeous man. He backed against the wall. *Sonofabitch, this is my nemesis? The guy who's going to rip the guts out of the Charm?*

"I am. Actually, I arrived a few minutes later than I expected since I couldn't find..."

"Yeah, anyway, welcome to the Southern Charm." He rose to his feet, twitched his shorts in place, then went to his room before the man could finish any explanations or issues with his home. At the door, he turned and stared at the slender man. *Change a damn thing and I'll wring your freaking neck.* "I'll get changed and be with you in the foyer in ten." With that last message, he slammed the door in Samuel's face. He could hear Samuel's dry response even through the heavy door.

"Nice to meet you too."

Ignoring the last dig by Samuel, Dakota tossed the towel toward the bathroom. He heard the door close next to him and stared at the wall where his bed rested. He groaned when he realized that Samuel would be sleeping next to him.

Hearing Samuel milling about, unpacking, and whatever, Dakota kicked off his board-shorts and flopped back on the bed. He debated whether to return to the shower or get dressed. Lowering his gaze, he stared at his rigid cock standing up and at attention without a barrier of cloth.

Sure he found Samuel annoying and stiff from this first bump and introduction, but everything else about him hit all the right buttons. As he thought about those melted caramel eyes, Dakota groaned and wrapped a fist around his penis. He masturbated slow and steady since he was close to orgasm. His mind brought up the rest of the image with the stylish honey-highlighted hair and pale cream skin. As a chef, his brain often connected food to colors and thoughts. It was annoying at times, but this time the colors fit the man.

Continuing to masturbate until he felt himself almost at the point of orgasm, Dakota stopped and released his hand from his penis. He reached back to the nightstand where a bottle of lube rested. His aching balls and cock yelled at him, but he ignored the urge to continue.

When the intense feeling of almost ejaculating subsided a bit, he poured lube on his palm and rubbed his hands together. He rubbed only the shaft without touching the head with two fingers. He continued to stimulate the shaft, pulling back as he got closer to hold back the orgasm, wanting it to grow.

He took time to concentrate on his movements along with the image of Samuel bent over him, adding his own touch. Circling and stroking the shaft, he breathed heavily as he approached the edge. He got real close and moved his hand less and less. When his hand was still, he took in heavy, deep breaths.

As he experimented and changed his breathing, the sensation altered within his balls. The ejaculation rose, and he held his breath. He tightened the muscles in his ass, thighs and further up his body.

Giving himself one, long, slow, firm stroke on the shaft, Dakota yelled at the power of the orgasm erupting. The explosive pumping of cum poured from the slit, falling onto his belly, as he let his entire body relax. Dropping an arm over his face as he breathed through the residual drop of endorphins, Dakota grinned at the feeling in his body.

He could only guess what Samuel was thinking next door. With a laugh, Dakota rolled off the bed to clean up and changed into khaki shorts and a printed T-shirt with sandals.

Dakota charged downstairs and through the back porch. He shoved open the screen door, stormed across the weathered wood deck, and leaned against the railing. He needed a few minutes to get his head wrapped around what was happening. Instead of standing motionless, he yearned to remove the stress by running along the beach for a few pounding miles.

Samuel Ashford was here before he'd fully wrapped his head about what was happening. Caught on the edge, Dakota knew he would scramble to catch up to what was happening. With one foot braced on the lower rung, he stared at the gentle waves breaking onto the wide expanse of empty beach. From the height of the waves and the spread of sand, he knew it was low tide. If he wanted, he could wade out far into the water and not go higher than his knees. He could dig for hours in the sand and come up with a bucketful of sand clams to turn into a delicious creation.

The noisy caws drew his attention up the beach. He studied a pair of seagulls fighting over something either left behind by beachgoers or what the tide had dragged up the sand. Other seagulls sat and watched from a lifeguard tower. Perhaps they waited out the fight before they dropped in for their piece of the action.

Dakota tried to recall when the beaches used to be full of visitors and locals lying back on the soft sand, browning and baking their brains under the hot sun, while others caroused in the water.

Damn hurricanes. Fucking Horizon. Screwed with my life right when I had what I wanted.

Hearing someone opening the door and the weathered cedar boards creaking under footsteps, he looked over his shoulder. He'd told Samuel they would meet in the foyer. What was he doing following him outside? Guilt washed over him. They hadn't exactly had a brilliant start. If he was to have a southern snowball's chance of keeping any of the Charm the way it was, he needed to keep on the offensive all wrapped up in a smile. Hating how he'd reacted up in the corridor at hearing Samuel's name, he decided to suck up his pride and take the first step to make amends.

"I think we should start again," he said.

Samuel watched him with a narrow-eyed gaze and an expression of concern. "Probably a good thing considering we need to work together for an unknown time."

Dakota held out his hand which Samuel shook. It was firm and short. Neither one tested the other's strength.

"I should apologize for knocking you to your feet. I was drying my hair and not paying attention to where I was going. In my defense, I didn't expect anyone on the floor." He gave Samuel the patented Dakota grin, but there wasn't a response.

"I was distracted by looking around the hall and wasn't watching either," Samuel admitted.

Finally Dakota shuffled from one foot to the other. "So, we should return to simple introductions for a new beginning. Agreed?"

"Agreed."

Swallowing to get past the curt answer, Dakota pulled in a deep breath to control his nerves. "I'm Dakota Mitchell. I'm the creator and chef of the restaurant, Southern Delights, located here at the Charm. As part of the original agreement, I'm also part owner of the B&B." The direction of the gentle wind changed and carried with it the scent of the sea, and the soft reminder was enough to put steel in his spine. "The sudden knowledge of the sale and my friends losing something they created for most of their lifetimes has been a shock. I don't do well at the business side of it all except for restaurant stuff. I'm better with food."

"Why only with food? How do you do well with only food and create a successful restaurant?"

"I don't bother much with the guests. I concentrate on handling the food, creating the dishes and menus, putting it together, balancing the look of the meal on a plate, running everything within the restaurant and stuff. As the chef, I prefer to stay in the kitchen where I belong."

Samuel looked around them in obvious answer then back to Dakota.

"Yes, I know. We're not there. It's why I'm screwing this up."

"Should we move to the kitchen?"

"It wouldn't help at this point, but I'm sure you'll need to give me multiple chances to fix my screw-ups. Figured you wanna be forewarned and all that." In an intentional repetition to enforce the new start, Dakota shoved his hand out between them. "Welcome to the Southern Charm, it's our little bit of paradise on the Gulf Coast."

After a lift of an eyebrow, Samuel shook hands once more. This time the grip lingered a little longer, a little harder. "Mr Mitchell…"

"It's Dakota, please, or Kota. My father is Mister and I'm far away from anything like him."

"Fine. Dakota. Samuel Ashford. I'm here to represent Ashford Hotels. Thank you for allowing us to help create this new venture with you."

"A new venture. Right, I guess we can see it from the point of view. It'll be a new start for the Southern Charm." Dakota swallowed. "It's a pleasure to meet you, Sam."

"Samuel."

"Excuse me?"

"My name is Samuel."

"Okay. Samuel." Dakota wondered if *Samuel's* tie was a little too tight around his neck. "What exactly is it you're going to do here during your stay?"

"I'm here to inspect the hotel, see how things work, and decide what we can do to improve."

Leaning back against the railing, Dakota crossed arms over his chest. "Improve? You mean change what makes the Charm special and into one of those cookie cutter hotels sporting your name." He raised a hand and shook a finger in Samuel's face. "Uh-huh, it's not happening with this place."

"You better get the finger out of my face if you wish for me to cooperate in any way," Samuel said, his voice tightened.

"What will happen if I don't comply with your demands?"

"I shut the hotel down for months to finish my corporation's investigation into the possibility of continuing operations or give it a permanent shutdown."

"You wouldn't dare do such a damn thing..."

"Try me," Samuel said.

"What the fuck stuck the stick up your ass?"

Samuel raised an eyebrow.

"Fine. Done," Dakota said as he shoved his hand in a pocket. "Happy?"

"I am now." Samuel tilted his head. "I believe you mentioned your distaste in change earlier. You were quite thorough in your concerns."

"No, not all changes. There is your type which removes anything unique and remarkable about the Charm or dares to threaten with shutting down the main source of income for the entire town. Our clients spread their valuable dollars throughout the town's shops and restaurants as well as the one here during their stay. We need the money from the Charm to keep this town alive."

"I don't believe this will be the case. There will be a thorough investigation into the books so I can figure out the best course of action. While the Charm will be the first amongst a unique collection of boutique style hotels for our chain, there will need to be updates and changes. Any change implemented here would result in direct cuts to overhead costs and would ultimately lead to an improvement in the bottom line." This was clearly Samuel's arena. He was animated, defensive and offensive and bristly with energy. Dakota wished he had half of the argument skills the other guy had.

"The Charm isn't all about bottom line. We're a special market hotel to entice our clients to enjoy the white sandy beaches and lazy lifestyle the Gulf offers. Take the bathrooms for instance." Dakota animatedly drew a shape in the air. "In there we offer local made soaps, hair cleansing products, and hand products all of which are environmental friendly. There are the beeswax candles, artwork and pottery. Local artists design and create these details. Would you want to change everything? Put out our artists who also prosper when clients visit them in their shops? And we put fresh flowers in every room." He dropped his hands and grumbled under his breath when Samuel stared at him like Dakota had killed a kitten. Or several kittens.

"Does the hotel offer this to every customer?" he asked brusquely.

"Every room, every customer, every time. It's a strict policy we keep for all guests since we opened the doors and established the connection to the town." Dakota counted each off on his fingers but all Samuel did was huff.

"It's a potential waste of money when you're barely in the black at the end of each month. I saw the basic financial statements, but you don't have the additional money to throw away on frivolous items." He was dismissing Dakota's impassioned speech like it was nothing.

Temper began to simmer in the pit of Dakota's stomach. "I don't agree," he said firmly. "The individuality is what the Charm is known and loved for by her regulars. It's the personal touches to bring the beauty of the Gulf into the hotel. Should I dare ask what is wrong with the Charm?"

Now it was Samuel's turn to count off on his fingers. "The signs from the road are horrendous, most travelers would never find this place either on a whim or if they're actually coming here. Even with a current map and updated GPS unit, I had difficulty finding this place. You have an outdated website with links to old news about the oil spill. There is the lack of marketing. I mean, do you have marketing of any sort newer than the nineties and wasn't created in Word using templates? The road is a horrendous mess. What is up with the gravel? There is the dilapidated gate and fence. And the fountain... There is green muck around the base and no water flow from the top. Why keep it?" Samuel motioned toward the Charm. "There is the building itself. It needs some work. Fresh paint, upgrades to the computer systems, security around the front desk, and new linens to start. I'll know more after I take a thorough search of all the rooms and the building itself."

Holy hell! Was there anything actually left Samuel did like? Dakota could immediately think of one thing. Though he was amazed at how fast Samuel's mouth and thoughts went when he got going on a subject he wanted. Part of it was attractive how cute Samuel became when he got heated. Dakota's cock certainly took notice.

"I mean, please, there is a lot to be changed."

"Is there anything you do like?"

Holding firm to his position in the argument, Samuel shook his head. "Not from my current point of view."

"It does have one of the finest seafood restaurants on the coast," he said and pointed a finger at Samuel.

"Do I need to remind you about the finger?"

"Sonofa... Really? You're going to go there?"

"I don't appreciate it."

Dakota moved his hands behind him and gripped the railing.

"As for the restaurant, it remains to be seen by me. You do have good reviews, but they are few on details. This includes the various financial statements which I'll need to look through and compare to various assets and expenses to verify the numbers." Samuel raised his eyebrows. "I'll need to see the menu. Do some kind of schedule program of tasting. We'll talk afterwards."

Dakota bristled. "There's no set menu."

"What do you mean there's no set menu? How do you plan the cost of a meal in advance and obtain economies in purchase?"

Checking out his fingers as if nonchalant, Dakota glanced at Samuel. "I use fresh, local produce, seafood, and order in specialty meats. I create the menu on whatever is in season or what I feel like making. I base the menu on the prices I received and turning them into the various dinners offered. I know what to charge each dish to maximize the amount of food. Sure, there are some items I continue from one day to the next, but I change most of the main dishes. Tonight, I'm having a seafood gumbo, fried clam platter, spiced lobster pasta, and a smoked tea chicken salad for the choices of the main dishes. There isn't a printed menu, but a blackboard I update at the entrance. We often keep the kitchen open until eleven or later, depending on the amount of customers and food. Other times we close the doors early and it all depends on what the folks want."

"How could you possibly know what makes money and what doesn't? This is no way to track the various dishes to see if they're monetarily successful versus the purchase price. You can't run a successful business like this."

"My restaurant is packed every evening." This time he pointed his finger straight up, spearing the air and not at the annoying Yankee. He added another finger as he ticked off the reasons for his restaurant's status. "Wait times are often up to two hours for a table at the height of the tourist season, but customers don't care. We have a great bar, good music out here on the patio, and a dance floor set on the sand. It's not about money. The Delights is the mainstay of the Charm. If it isn't a success, you're clearly blind and there isn't any point in you being here."

"Wait, wait, wait a moment," Samuel said and waved a hand to halt him. "Did you tell me it's booked out every night?"

"Every single damn night. Every single damn table and more," Dakota said with a pause between each word to make his point sharp.

"Why is the restaurant running at a loss when I look through the accounts and financial statements? Sometimes there is a significant loss with no explanation."

"It has to be an accounting error." *Full tables meant money. Samuel was wrong.*

"I may not be a numbers man, but they don't lie when I checked and rechecked. You're hemorrhaging money like a colander leaks water."

Dakota didn't have a comeback. Instead he decided he was way past being patient and turned to making Samuel uncomfortable. There's only one way to screw with a straight guy's head.

He stepped into Samuel's space, wrapped his fingers around the base of the man's skull, and yanked him up on his toes. He planted a hard, deep kiss on those intriguing, damning lips. "Come and try me out." After releasing the man, he brushed against Samuel's shoulder in a light, deliberate fashion as he strolled back toward the Charm. Okay, so it wasn't the most professional of closures to the meeting but hell, his kitchen was waiting.

"In your dreams," Samuel muttered.

Dakota grumbled when he caught the muttering. *What is it with the stuffy Yankee and his having the last word?*

Chapter Four

Samuel pressed his fingers to his mouth, finding it puffy from the harsh kiss. In spite of Dakota's infernal attitude, he wanted another kiss. He flexed his hands a few times at the irony between finding it impossible to talk to Dakota—stubborn as all get out—and wanting to yank him close. There was the damn annoyance of getting a finger pointed in his face. But the heat and passion was in the kiss. Dakota wanted to piss him off, but it fired the passion within him. Samuel blew out a long breath.

No matter how gorgeous Dakota was, there was no way this could work. No matter how much he wanted another kiss, Dakota was impossible, arrogant, and sexy as all hell. Dakota would fight him at every turn, suggestion and change. They would snap and argue at each other for every inch, during every hour, and about every fucking item for the entire time he stayed here. Nothing would happen and the Charm would fail. He would fail.

"I will not fail. Not my first time. I *will* make this damn plan work. I will *not* fail," he muttered. "Forget another kiss. No more kissing."

Deciding to match Dakota head on with his own game, Samuel studied his business-like outfit, perfect for the office in New York. Since he'd joined the upper echelon of his family's company, he decided to alter his clothing from the strict business attire. It would be the first time since he'd accepted his current position to appear anywhere out of a full suit. No matter their location, time or position, an Ashford always presented themselves to the highest accord. Still, he needed to conform somewhat to his surroundings if he wanted things to work. He undid the golden cufflinks, dropped them in a pocket, and rolled both sleeves up his forearms. He yanked off the tie, shoved the Hermès blue patterned heavy silk into the same pocket, and undid the first few buttons.

With a spreading out of his fingers while pushing them down and away to calm his breathing, arousal and irritation, he followed Dakota back inside and found his way into the busy kitchen. It gleamed with stainless steel, bamboo and granite. There were several large walk-in cold units, a pair of huge stoves, a large charcoal grill, a flat-top grill and so many other things he couldn't determine a use. It seemed to be set in some kind of specific pattern, but he wasn't sure.

The scents, though…

He pulled in a deep breath to catch all the delicious aromas and almost moaned with pleasure.

"You. What the hell are you doing in here? You're in my way if you stay there," Dakota called out, yanking Samuel's attention from pleasure and back to reality. "Move it."

Samuel turned and saw Dakota stalking him, his lower body draped with a pristine white apron and towel.

"You haven't given me a tour."

"Look around you. I'm a little busy and don't have time to give a tour. Wander around on your damn time, not mine. Stay out of my kitchen. I have food to prepare for hungry people." Dakota waved a hand at him to leave and returned to the stoves and a large pot.

"There's time to show him around, Kota. We'll finish here," one of the male assistants said.

"Malcolm, please, you need to butt out. This is none of your concern," Dakota said.

"If he's the new owner..." The handsome reddish-brunet male turned from a large tub of chicken breasts covered with some kind of dark fragrant liquid. Samuel noticed the man colored the tips of his hair with a bright blue.

"Co-owner," Dakota said in a stiff, tight tone.

"Fine. You're a co-owner. Jeez." Malcolm rolled his eyes over the sharp distinction. "You should show him around our establishment and point out all the wonders of our little slice of heaven. Though, he is cute. I could show him around by myself." Malcolm grinned and waved in Samuel's direction. "Hi there, cutie."

Samuel smiled at Malcolm's flirtation.

"Knock it off, Mal. He doesn't care about the wonders, only the problems." Dakota leaned against the counter as he stared at Samuel. "Why should I bother?"

"Call it plain and simple southern hospitality. Now move your fine ass. I'll cover things until you return," the sous chef said with a nod to Samuel.

"Damn waste of my time, but I'll take him around." Dakota's movements were sharp as he yanked off the apron and slapped it down on a stool.

"Nicely," Malcolm said. "I want you to be nice to him. Remember what I said — southern hospitality!"

"Hospitality, right, at least I haven't tossed him in the ocean." Dakota grumbled as he went passed Samuel. "Follow me."

Samuel nodded back to the chef in thanks for his assistance. "A pleasure to meet you," he said. "Since he forgot the introduction, I'm Samuel Ashford."

"Nice to meet you, Samuel, and it wouldn't be the first time he neglected the basic courtesies and manners. Malcolm Bissette, but you can call me Mal. I'm the battered, hounded assistant and sous chef to the maestro. If he doesn't behave, you have my permission to whack him. Come on back and see me anytime, handsome," he said with a laugh and wiggle of his fingers.

"Shut it, Mal. Don't let the chicken dry out!" Dakota said with a bark to his tone.

"It's drunk on tea. I don't think it'll be a problem."

A chuckle escaped as Samuel turned to follow Dakota. He tugged his iPhone from his pocket to make notes during the tour. "Note to self. Initial tour of Southern Charm with co-owner Dakota Mitchell," he said to the phone. He banged into a solid form and stopped short. "You gotta stop doing that." After a shake of his head, he stared at the muscular back covered in soft cotton. "Why did you stop?"

"Are you going to talk to a phone the entire time?" Dakota turned to stare at the phone.

"I need to make notes so I can figure out what's going on with the Charm."

"Do the freaking walk-through with me first. Okay? I don't want to hear you yapping the entire time. It'll be a frigging waste of my time. We're on a time crunch since I have customers coming within the next couple of hours and I have to feed them. I need to return to the kitchen after I show you where everything is around here. I'll leave you on your own devices. You can look at everything and make your" — he waved at the phone—"precious notes to your heart's content."

Samuel held up his hands. "Okay. Though it isn't how I wish to deal with things, since my preference is recording my first impressions. To keep things civil between us, I'll concede to your request and put it away." He slid the phone back in his pocket after shutting it off.

Dakota shoved a hand through his hair, messing the layers. The curls fell around his face in a tempting fashion. In spite of their tangled arguments, Samuel wanted to reach out and smooth back one of those soft-looking locks.

"Where do we start on this nickel tour? Or are we dropping it down to a penny's worth?"

Without answering, Dakota turned and went down the short hallway away from the kitchen. He leaned against the wall and waved a hand.

"Okay. A penny." Samuel looked around and followed.

"We'll start this way." Dakota pointed to the various doors on either side. "Our two offices are here. The one on this side is mine," he said and thumbed at the door behind him. He pointed a finger across the hall. "This office belonged to Edward and is yours while you're here."

Stepping over, Samuel looked into the offices, noting the heavy dark wood furniture and computers, but there was little in way of storage or filing except the multiple stacks of cardboard boxes. The large desks covered in piles of paperwork and folders. In Dakota's chosen office, he spotted a large corkboard stretched along one wall with pictures of food, and papers tacked to it.

"What's on the board?" He glanced over at Dakota, intrigued by the amount of paperwork.

"Recipes, ideas, meal plans, and other things I want to try out. Some are orders or lists of items I need to remind myself. I deal with all the kitchen stuff with my assistant, Malcolm, and the hostess, Cecile, manages the front staff. Mal's the pain in the ass you met in the kitchen, but I put up with him. Otherwise I have to handle all the paperwork, and I hate the stuff."

"What about Edward?"

"Edward had an assistant, a bookkeeper, who dealt with the books in the small side office, which has a connecting doorway."

"So, there are three offices back here?"

"I call them two and half."

Samuel smiled at the quiet joke. "Is this bookkeeper here today? What is his name?"

"No. He works part-time on Wednesdays. His name is Thomas. Thomas Harding."

"Does he come in on other days if needed?"

Dakota shook his head. "He's in his other office downtown for the rest of the time. He's only here the one morning to go through the books."

"Does he do the restaurant books?"

"Yes."

"Hmm." Samuel wondered if he would find the issue of discrepancies with Thomas' work with the books.

"Why do you ask?"

"Something I wish to look into further before discussing with you."

"Ahh, that's such a non-answer, but okay. Sure, whatever you wish to do."

"What else is there on this tour?"

"You want more?" Dakota pointed at a door. "Through the swing door down there at the end of the hall is the employee area, the laundry room and storage area. Want to see it?"

"Perhaps, I would like to see the main areas first and get a feel of the place. As you mentioned, I'll wander around more on my own later."

With a nod, Dakota shoved a hand into his pocket, brushed past Samuel, and left the hallway. Samuel pulled in a breath when Dakota's hip moved against him. He snagged hold of Dakota's waistband and stopped him. He lifted his gaze and met Dakota's stare.

Neither man moved an inch, keeping the faint connection between them.

"What are you doing, Yankee?"

"I..." Samuel moved his gaze to Dakota's lips.

"Want another kiss?"

"I heard you earlier..."

"What did you hear?"

"You were masturbating."

"Did you like listening to my private moment?"

Samuel flushed, but kept his gaze upon Dakota. "Yeah, I would like it better if you thought about me while you got yourself off."

"You were on my mind. Your eyes remind me of melted caramels." Dakota traced a finger around the edge of the bone structure surrounding Samuel's eyes. "I was ready to blow after tangling with you."

"Did you enjoy yourself?"

"I yelled when I came. I came hard. I want to kiss you again. Give me something else for my fantasies." Dakota dragged a finger along Samuel's lower lips. He ran his tongue over Samuel's lip, slipped in against his sensitive gums, the edge of his teeth, reached to the top of his mouth. He pulled back to keep their lips together, moist and demanding.

Samuel slid his fingers into Dakota's hair. He groaned when they shifted, and Dakota pressed him against the nearest wall. Dakota shoved a thigh between Samuel's legs, grabbing his ass and lifting him until their thick cocks met.

Dakota kissed him hard and deep, but broke away to lean back. "This is too damn dangerous for us to mix our relationships." He released his grip, lowered Samuel to the ground, and stepped away. He cleared his throat and broke the connection.

Trying to figure out how to breathe again, Samuel relied on the wall to keep him upright. He dragged air into his needy lungs. Confused about the man and the odd feelings he brought up, Samuel remained in place when Dakota moved away. What he would do next with the recalcitrant chef, he wasn't sure. He shoved fingers through his hair and pressed his other hand against his erection irritated by the zipper.

"Are you coming?"

"I want to."

Dakota lifted an eyebrow. "I meant the tour. There is more than this hallway."

"Yes, I know, need another look," Samuel said as he studied Edward's office in a mask to take extra moments to control his body.

"Any day now…"

Appeasing the irritated chef, Samuel pushed away from the wall and followed him. His eyes dropped to Dakota's lean ass. He wanted to take hold of it. Instead, he forced himself to maintain composure and concentrated on his job.

Over the next half hour, Dakota continued the impromptu tour and pointed out the front entry, the small library with a gorgeous stone fireplace lit with a series of candles, a living room area with comfortable furniture arranged to encourage conversations, and a special room certified to be accessible to those guests with physical disabilities, known as the ADA room. After the ADA room, they went upstairs to look through some of the available rooms. Samuel noticed Dakota made sure to point out all the local influence in every area, from the bathroom items, floral arrangements, decorations, and other simple things. He gritted his teeth as Dakota hounded on the local touch and knew the man wouldn't let it go.

When they made their way downstairs, Dakota stopped by the hostess station in front of the elegant double-door entrance. Beyond the doors was the recently upgraded dining room. The glass beautifully engraved on both doors with the Delights' name and logo.

Samuel stopped and touched the glass. "This is gorgeous. Where did you find this?"

"A local glass artist, Wyatt McBride, designed it. He helped install them with the local carpenter-handyman from town."

Great, now I have a pair of local heroes to deal with in this place.

"He did excellent work."

"Hmm. Folks in expensive galleries appreciate his work."

"What galleries?"

"Don't know their names. Some places in New York, Chicago and San Francisco. He sells his stuff all over, but keeps his base here."

"Did he grow up here?"

"No, he's a transplant from somewhere in Pennsylvania. He visited for a break, to see what he needed to do in life and art, and ended up buying a place."

"It sounds like he's a good friend."

"He is and often comes to the restaurant." Dakota ended the conversation and opened one of the doors. "Here's the main restaurant. We expanded it ten years ago and gave it a fresh coat of paint and interior change about five years ago."

"It's a good use of the space, a lot of light from the front windows, and a good atmosphere."

"Those windows are actually all on tracks like large barn doors. We can open all of them with full access to the porch where we could set additional tables, an outdoor bar, a fire pit, and a small stage where we have local bands play when the weather is nice."

"Must be nice to listen too, watch, and eat," Samuel said. "You can see all the way to the water."

"Hmm, it's a clear view down the beach. Something I made sure to keep when working on the renovations with Sully."

"Sully?"

"He's the local carpenter-handyman who built this new space."

"Another local person, I see. Can he work on an entire building?"

"He's a licensed contractor, but prefers the simpler work of carpentry or handyman stuff. If you're interested, you can give him a call and see what he says. He's fixed little stuff here and there for the price of a meal."

"It's an interesting exchange of work."

"He likes my cooking," Dakota said with a shrug. "The tour is done. I need to return to the kitchen."

Four people walked through the swinging doors. Two of them carried baskets filled with various items while two others carried khaki colored tablecloths. All four wore jeans and khaki colored shirts with the restaurant's logo on the upper chest and back. One waiter with lanky brown hair stared at them, not concentrating on his work.

"Who are they?" Samuel asked as he waved at the workers.

Dakota turned to look over at the waiters. "They're some of the waiters for the dinner shift. They come in and set all the tables before we open the doors, clean things down, and pre-set all of the utensils wrapped in their cloth napkins."

"Is this their usual uniform?"

"Yes, we provide them with three short-sleeve shirts, two long-sleeve shirts, and a ball-cap upon signing up with us. Everything has the restaurant's logo embroidered on the cloth. We give them a white apron, which they'll use for the service. The rest is up to them, but there are standards."

"Dakota... Dakota...how are you? I heard about what happened. I'm sorry about Edward. He was one of the hearts of this place," the waiter said as he raced over to Dakota's side. He placed a hand on Dakota's hip and leaned in closer.

"Hello, Allan, yes he'll be missed around here. I didn't know you were back in town," Dakota said as he moved Allan's hand with a deliberate two-fingered hold and drop.

Allan's eager look dropped. Stepping closer to lean against Dakota's side, he didn't lose his smile for long. "I gave school a try for a few semesters, but didn't like it. So I came back to stay with my brother and figure stuff out. Can I come and see you tonight?"

After the heated kiss they'd shared in the hall, Samuel gritted his teeth at how this kid draped himself over Dakota. He cleared his throat, unable to believe the gall of this kid. "Hello. I'm Samuel, the new co-owner of the Charm."

The kid gave him one of the dirtiest looks. "Allan. I'm one of the best waiters. How dare you buy the Charm from underneath Dakota? Do you know what he put into this place? His life. His heart…"

"Allan, enough," Dakota said.

"But, Dakota… You shouldn't have to put up with someone who has no idea what the Charm means…"

"Enough, you need to go back to the tables."

Allan shot another glare at Samuel, turned, then flounced off.

Samuel lifted an eyebrow at the kid's horrendous attitude. "What the hell is his issue?"

"We had a fling and he disappeared. I didn't know he was back. I need to speak with Malcolm and Cecile."

"Now he wants more," Samuel said. "He's a little pissed I'm standing here."

"Not everyone knew about the sale."

"Will I have a problem with them?"

"Depends on what you decide. I need to get to work."

"I'll go with you."

"I don't think so. You'll get in the way," Dakota said as he went through the restaurant toward the swinging doors.

Samuel was tight on his heels, determined to not let the man out of his sight. "I think I'll stay. I want to see how this place works."

Dakota growled under his breath.

"Did he behave himself like a southern gentleman? Do I need to whack his behind with a wooden spoon?" Malcolm moved around a corner, a container in his hands which he set on his workspace.

"Barely, but we can avoid the spanking. At least this time around, but keep the option open for a future time," Samuel said with a grin at the flirting chef. He didn't dare mention the heated kiss.

Malcolm hooted out a laugh. "He's got you cornered, boss."

Dakota glared at his sous chef before he snatched up the pristine apron, pulled it over his head, and tied it in place. At the small sink, he scrubbed and rinsed his hands in a thorough fashion. As he dried his hands on a paper towel, he gave Samuel a look. He pointed to a low table with a single chair. "If you want to watch, go there. Sit. Don't move and get in my way."

Samuel looked at the corner spot. "Are you kidding me?"

"You want to stay. You follow my rules. This is my kitchen with my rules."

"Rules of the chef, huh?"

"If you don't, you get whipped with a towel and hollered at," another one of Dakota's assistants said with a grin. He was an older man with graying hair at his temples and laugh lines spreading from his dark eyes. "Nice to meet you, Mr Ashford, I'm Glenn, the seafood line cook."

"Shut it, Glenn. Get back to cleaning those clams. I want them cleaned and battered and ready to roll for the orders."

"Yes, Chef," Glenn said and turned back to the huge colander of scrubbed, purged of grit, whole-belly steamer clams. He shucked them and poured the *clam liquor* in a bowl. After a quick toss of the shells, he dropped the flesh in a bowl. He glanced at another line cook working at a different prep station. "Don't let those lobsters crawl away from you, Dorian."

Dorian smacked a red shell right between those beady eyes. He batted the crustacean back from its valiant attempt to crawl out of the large wooden box. "Got it, stupid bugger doesn't want to be dinner."

Dakota shook his head at the chaos which came with live seafood.

Dorian pulled out a large red lobster. It wiggled its banded claws to show it was still alive. Samuel squeaked in shock when Dorian held it down on the table, shoved the knife point into the head and sliced it in half. The lobster stopped moving. Samuel swallowed hard and stared at the unmoving claw.

"If you're squeamish, you need to leave," Dakota said with a wicked grin.

"I'm not... What is he...?" Samuel waved a hand at the lobster killer.

"He's preparing lobsters in a humane way to kill them," Dakota said.

"He just... He..."

"Is shoving a knife in their brain and killing the lobsters, yes. It's one way you prepare the crustaceans.

Two other ways are shoving them into a freezer or dropping them in a boiling pot."

"Alive?"

"Yes, everything is done while they're alive to kill them. The knife stops all brain activity."

"I believe lobster tail will be off my diet for a bit." A little wobbly, Samuel swallowed hard, and sat down hard in the chair. He dragged a hand over his face. Dakota plunked a glass in front of him.

"Drink. You need it."

Samuel blinked at the tall chef in his pristine white apron. "What is it?"

"It isn't poisoned, I can assure you. It's traditional sun tea. A favorite of the South, sweetened with honey, and fresh mint added."

"I didn't ask..."

"Drink before you pass out."

"I'm not going to pass out." Samuel glanced at the lobster killer, winced as the knife sliced another red shelled head, then he drank half of the glass. He caught the sweetened mint iced tea taste. "Holy... This is good."

"It's one of our specialty drinks. We brew gallons of it fresh everyday out in the sun on one of the upper decks to catch all the sunlight it needs. The mint is grown locally along with the honey from local bees."

"How do you brew this in the sun?"

"You never had traditional sun tea?"

Samuel shook his head.

"It's a Southern thing. You don't know everything the South can offer. Are you allergic to anything?"

Dazed by the change of topic, Samuel nodded. "Nuts."

"Nuts? Any kind of nuts?"

"Peanuts, hazelnuts, walnuts..." Samuel shrugged. "I learned to avoid all of them since I was a kid and all their varieties like oils and stuff. I was one of those kids who could never have a peanut butter sandwich. They do bad things to me."

"How bad of a reaction are we talking about?"

"It could be life threatening if there is a big enough dose." He tugged out a small EpiPen from his pocket. "I can't leave home without this."

"Do you go into anaphylactic shock?"

"Yes." Samuel pushed the injector back in his pocket. "This gives me a measured shot of epinephrine to counteract the worst of the symptoms and allows enough time to get my ass either in an ambulance or be driven to the nearest hospital."

Allan paused as he entered the kitchen to listen to the conversation. He skipped over and grinned at Dakota. "Hey there, Dakota..."

"Allan? What are you doing in here? It's getting close to the dinner shift. You're here as a food runner, not a server, and we need to get everything ready," Dakota asked.

"I know my position, but I was free when Cecile wanted to know the house specials. She sent me in to ask you for the list," Allan said.

"Did you ask or volunteer?" Samuel muttered.

Allan gave him a nasty glare, but smiled back to Dakota.

"As procedure, I'll bring the list to her," Dakota said.

"Oh, it used to be I can ask you for the list. I'm sorry, I didn't know about the changes."

"It changed a few months ago. There was no reason for you to come in and let the others set the tables. As you can see, I'm a little busy right now and they need you in the dining room to finish preparations."

"Okay, I'm sorry to intrude. I wanted to help. Bye, Dakota." Allan gave him a light wave and left.

"Yes, there is something wrong here. I don't like him," Samuel said.

"You're not in charge of my restaurant. It falls under my fifty percent control."

"Whatever you wish, but know I don't appreciate his attitude."

"It'll be noted as a concern." Dakota shoved a hand through his hair and shook his head. "As for your allergy issue, there are no uses of nuts in tonight's dishes. Have you eaten?"

"A few hours ago, I found something quick while I was on the road from the airport. Of course I had a meal on the flight."

"What I thought, airline food is nuked crap no matter what they do to change it."

Dakota stirred whatever was in the big pot and grabbed a ladle. He poured a generous helping into a bowl, snagged a spoon, a few slices of crusty bread, and served Samuel at the corner table. "Eat."

Samuel stared down at the bowl then lifted his gaze to Dakota, who seemed to make it his mission to drive him bonkers. "What is it?"

"My seafood gumbo and it's renowned amongst favorites and critics this far from the bayou. I did manage to get with various Cajuns and Creoles to learn a few secrets while I spent a few years in New Orleans."

"Gumbo?" Samuel used the spoon to pick and poke at the thickened concoction. "What's in it?"

"Four different kinds of seafood, vegetables, and spices, but anything more would be giving away secrets. Eat." The chef walked off to begin preparations for the rest of the offered meals with the finishing touches to be done upon receiving orders.

After another cautious poke, Samuel scooped a little on the edge of his spoon and tried a taste. He moaned with absolute pleasure, as if he'd hit a food orgasm.

Shit, the man was a damn good chef.

Chapter Five

The kitchen ramped up in activity as the evening rush filled the restaurant. Dakota gave Samuel several glares, but he remained in place. He couldn't help himself. The chef was interesting and it was hot to watch him in full control. Samuel shifted his cock to relieve the pressure in his pants. Now he wanted to go upstairs and masturbate to all the heated fantasies Dakota drew in his mind. He almost orgasmed when he heard Dakota's pleasured shout through the wall.

After another annoyed stare from Dakota, Samuel figured he got a sense of how the kitchen ran, and moved out of the way. After a quick trip out to his car, he grabbed hold of the two suitcases, but left the garment bag of suits. When he kept hearing of the fashion sense around here, he didn't want to feel completely out of place. He carried his bags upstairs and heaved them onto the bed.

Blowing out a long breath, Samuel wiped the sweat off his forehead. "Man... Okay, need to see about getting someone to help bring up the damn bags. There are too many stairs in this place. We need a freaking elevator." He dropped on the bed, wiped at his damp neck and groaned again. "Too damn hot." Rising, he stood underneath the nearest vent, pulled at the back of his shirt to remove it from his sticky back, and moaned as the cool air rushed over him. "Ahh. Bliss."

Though, he couldn't stay there all night. Digging into his pocket, he dropped off his tie and cufflinks on the small dresser. He heaved the main suitcase to the rack, flipped open the suitcase and dug out a short-sleeved linen shirt. Tucking in the tails, he grumbled when he saw how the front of his pants looked and adjusted his cock. He dragged his fingers through his styled hair. A check confirmed he appeared decent, relaxed, but in command. He removed his heavier shoes, damp socks, and found a pair of lightweight loafers for a little more comfort. Finding the folder of information and computer case, he slung the strap over his shoulder and headed downstairs.

As he passed the front entry and the restaurant entrance, he whistled low at the number of people standing there. As Dakota boasted, the line of customers was impressive. A young petite lady with café au lait skin and a flourish of curly black hair manned the hostess station with ease and confidence. She wore the same embroidered shirt, but glammed it up with a black skirt and a rich printed scarf wrapped around her hair. Though she was barely five-five in height, everyone appeared to listen and follow her commands.

Winding his way through the crowd, Samuel stopped next to the station. He waited as she tapped her ear and voice mike combination before lifting her gaze to him and smiling.

"Good evening, I'm the hostess, Cecile," she said in a voice filled with the Creole accent normally heard in New Orleans.

Her accent and warm amber eyes entranced Samuel along with the natural warmth and charm. "Welcome to Southern Delights. I apologize but it'll be at least a half hour wait or more tonight. Would you like to put your name on the list? We have an outdoor bar and seating area where you can wait and enjoy a cocktail and appetizers."

"It's nice to meet you, Cecile. I'm Samuel Ashford, the new co-owner, and I don't need a reservation. Chef Dakota already gave me some food during my visit to the kitchen. The gumbo is divine. I require a little information from you," he said with an answering smile.

"Things are a little busy here, this evening." She blinked and a little frost covered her expression. "Are you from the Ashford chain?"

Samuel nodded.

"Dakota mentioned you arrived earlier than expected. He said to help you however we could."

"Really? Did he mention anything else?"

"You're looking around and making notes," she said. "You shouldn't change much. No one will come to the Charm."

"No one is coming to the Charm."

"They're coming to the Delights."

"I can see, but they're not extending their stay. I hope to alter this problem for the better." Samuel stopped and pulled his eyebrows together at something she'd said earlier. "Did you say a half hour wait? Is this normal for a Thursday?"

"It'll increase as the night continues and we're in the offseason. In the height of the season, we're over a two hour wait, but no one minds or causes problem. They know the food will be some of the finest Gulf shore seafood."

"Quite a reputation for this place," he said as he looked around.

"A reason people stop in town is to find us."

"But the signs to find the Charm are horrid."

"They manage to find us every night." She lifted the pad with a list of names and times. "May I get back to our customers?"

"Thank you for all your assistance."

Samuel poked his head in the kitchen and saw Dakota moving around, in complete control of what looked like utter chaos.

"Not now, Ashford," Dakota said.

Samuel blinked and leaned back. He didn't think the man would know he was there, but damn... *He's good. He's one helluva interesting man even if he is stubborn and pig-headed. One hell of a kisser, shit, Samuel, get it off your mind. No kissing him.* He entered the office where Edward had sat until this morning, placed his laptop bag and file down, settled in the chair, and found an envelope addressed to 'Ashford' waiting on the top of a pile.

Inside there was a letter welcoming him in a warmer fashion than he'd received since his arrival. Accompanying the letter, he found a list of accounts, phone numbers, and passwords for vendors along with the log-on information for the dragon of a computer. There was the information he needed about Thomas Harding, the assistant and bookkeeper. He circled and starred the information. He hit the button. Loud noises clattered and clanked as the computer went through a laborious boot-up process.

Amazed at the ancient piece of equipment, Samuel pulled out his iPhone, iPad and laptop and turned them all on. All had fully booted up before the old desktop had even made it to the welcome screen. He gathered some of the piles on the desk together to make room. He opened a new document on his laptop and transcribed notes from his phone to it about the exterior recommendations and added interior ones.

"New computer network overhaul for back offices and front desk. Need an updated lockbox program for room keys. Work on filing system in main office including purchase of various cabinets and organization materials," he said while he typed. "Figure out about this Harding guy and the books. Give the books a thorough read-through. Suggest to Dakota about a request to contact Chandler. Need Chandler to help out down here, it's right up his alley of crazy numbers not matching. Create list for mandatory fixes to structure, utilities, and rooms and find a local contractor and landscaper." There were a lot of basics that needed figuring out before he could deal with the aesthetics and details. At least to get the Charm updated and matching to what all the other Ashford hotels offered.

When the computer opened the log-on screen, Samuel shook his head, found the notes, and typed in the required password. He needed to wait longer for the next process. Once the desktop appeared, he flipped through the various files and programs. Most of the programs would need updating along with everything else. He scanned through some of the paperwork on the desk. He wrote notes on a legal pad in long-hand and typed in additional ones in the laptop to clean and focus on what he wanted. Altogether, he had to figure out the first pieces of information he needed to cull together for a report to his parents.

"Did you want something else from me?"

Startled by Dakota's voice, Samuel blinked his sore eyes. He rubbed his fingers over them. He looked up from the computers at the handsome chef, covered with the sheen of sweat across his face and neck. The man took long gulps from a glass of sun tea.

"Pardon? What did you ask?"

"You stopped outside the kitchen again and poked your head around the corner. Are you checking me out again? Thought you needed something else. Never mind, it's nothing important." Dakota shrugged a shoulder, placed a second glass of tea on the desk. "I figured you might need this. Do you have enough computers around you?"

"You didn't need to bring it to me, but I appreciate the gesture," Samuel said as he lifted the glass and took a long sip. "This is wonderful tea. I need the information from the desktop, but the others are my personal and company ones."

Dakota moved to sit on the edge of the desk after pushing a few piles aside.

Samuel glanced down at Dakota's long leg that helped brace him against the desk. Light blonde hairs covered the powerful thigh. Checking out the thigh wasn't enough—Samuel glanced at the bulge behind the zipper. After he licked his lower lip to hold back a moan, he dropped his stare to the glass.

"Samuel...Samuel..."

Samuel lifted his gaze to find Dakota staring at him with a raised eyebrow.

"You didn't hear a word I said."

"No, sorry. I'll pay attention."

Nicole Dennis

Dakota kept his eyebrow lifted high. "Are you sure? I can leave if you don't want to talk."

"No, no, I'm fine. Continue."

"I was only wondering about something."

"About what?"

"Why do you need all of them?" He picked up and moved a few pieces of paper, checked on a few of them, while he sipped his tea.

"All of what?"

Dakota waved a hand at the various electronics.

"Oh, these," Samuel said as he glanced at one muscular thigh.

After a few moments of more silence, Dakota leaned over, twitched his shorts to change Samuel's view, and tapped his fingers against Samuel's arm. "Samuel?"

Caught, Samuel lifted his gaze and flushed. Dakota's fingers slid against his skin. His thumb circled the sensitive area of Samuel's inner wrist. The touch seemed to go straight to his cock.

Dakota leaned closer with a smile. He moved his finger to brush Samuel's lower lip in a sensual, apparently deliberate fashion to knock him off axis. "So soft..."

"What..." Samuel lifted his gaze to meet Dakota's intense stare.

Clearing his throat, Dakota dropped his hand, stood, then moved away from the desk. "Nothing. Sorry. Damn shiny distracting moment."

"Squirrel?"

Dakota chuckled. "Yeah, I had a squirrel moment. Do you get them?"

"Sometimes."

"Why would you need both a laptop and an iPad? Couldn't you do the work with one or the other?"

Samuel swallowed hard at the loss of touch and change. "I use the Charm's one to figure out what is going on around here. I use mine to create and collate the information and notes before I pass them on to my company. Why do you ask?"

"It's interesting to see all of them. I know Edward wasn't the best at keeping things organized, not as much as he should. Perhaps we wouldn't be in the situation we're in if he kept better track of invoices and receipts and other information. I know he relied a lot upon Thomas, but I'm not sure about the man."

"Do you mean Thomas?"

"Yeah, he's not open and explaining things with me. I never saw detailed reports. I was going to speak with Edward about finding someone else to audit the books."

"I'm finding the disarray of the information for myself. I plan on ordering an audit as part of my thorough review of everything."

"Is there anything else I can do for you? Did you want something else? Coffee or food? We have a couple of leftovers, not much though. It was a busy night and we portioned everything well."

"No. No. I wanted to check out the kitchen when it was in full swing. Are you on a break?"

Dakota lifted an eyebrow and looked at the wall behind Samuel. He nodded toward it.

"What?"

"Do you know what time it is?"

"I've been working, not paying attention to the time."

"It's almost midnight. Everything I made lasted longer than I thought so we stayed open longer. Cecile and Malcolm are tallying up all the receipts and payments for the night. The staff is cleaning and sanitizing the kitchen under Glenn's guidance, but everyone is familiar with the procedures."

"Midnight? It can't be possible, nah, no way." Samuel narrowed his gaze at the bottom of his laptop screen. "Oh, damn, it is that late. I can't believe I've been in here that long."

"You hadn't noticed?"

Samuel shook his head. "I've been going through the paperwork and my notes."

"Yeah, I figured when I saw the light. The hotel closes down for the most part except we have a round-the-clock watch on the front desk for unexpected guests, who decide they no longer want to keep driving."

"Do you get a lot of walk-ins?"

"There are different times, yes. We learned to keep one or two smaller bedroom suites available. They get used at some point."

"Sit, please, I'm sure you must be tired," Samuel said with a wave to the chair.

"What? Don't want me on the desk again?"

"No, please, you disturbed…"

"You?"

Samuel cleared his throat which tightened with arousal. "No, the paperwork I've organized into specified piles to handle and review." He reached out and readjusted the papers Dakota had moved earlier. Gathering a second pile, he tapped the pages together though they didn't need it.

"Come on. It's more than the paperwork."

"Please, I don't believe it's appropriate. We checked each other out. As you pointed out, it's late and been a long, rough day." Samuel picked up the glass and took a long, grateful sip of the delicious liquid to quench his dry throat. "If you wish to speak about other things, please take a seat. What else is happening with the kitchen other than the final cleaning?"

With a glance over his shoulder to check the hallway, Dakota dropped in the chair. "Cecile finishes tallying the night's receipts with Malcolm as a witness and they pass out any final tips. It could take up to a half hour, depending on how the night went. If you don't mind, I can wait with you. I put the full pouch in the safe here."

"Is there a safe here?"

With a groan having just sat down, Dakota pushed back to his feet and went to the wall behind Samuel's chair. He revealed the simple hidden catch under the picture frame and helped it swing out to reveal the large wall safe with a keypad and fingerprint pad. "Here it is. This is something I insisted with the dual entrance pads."

Samuel stared at the large safe and glanced through the letter and notes from Edward. "I have the code he meant for the safe, but my print wouldn't work."

"No, we'll have to call the company to have you entered in the system and Edward removed." Dakota moved the painting back in place. Walking back, he trailed his fingers along Samuel's back. He flopped in the chair and linked his fingers behind his head.

"Something else to add to my list," Samuel muttered as he made a note on his laptop.

"What else is on the list?"

"I would like to call in an accountant who works with our corporation. He specializes in both forensic and current laws. As you suspected, I'm seeing a few things amongst the receipts and books and not comfortable with them."

"What are you seeing?"

"Numbers aren't lining up the way you would expect, but I started my foray into the books. I could be wrong. Either way, I would like to request for the bookkeeper to not work on the books until my company's accountant can look at these issues."

"So I could be right about Thomas. Do you think he did something to our books?"

"I'm seeing some evidence of misconduct, but again, this isn't my expertise. I would prefer to have Chandler look at everything before I make a definite answer. Would you mind if I asked him to come down here?"

Shoving a hand through his tangled hair, floppy from sweat and heat, Dakota let out a rumble of anger. "No, I would like to clear up the reasons behind why the restaurant is losing money when we have a packed house every night. I'll talk to Thomas and tell him not to come for a couple of weeks since we're working through new management. I want to hear his reaction and any protests he'll come up with to make an appearance."

"I would like to hear what Thomas has to say, but I'll wait until I have proof."

"I don't want any accusations flying around without proof." Groaning at what they were facing, Dakota dragged his hands down his face. "Call your guy and tell him to come down. I want to know what's happening and why we're losing money. What's his name? Is he really good at this numbers stuff?"

"Good. Thank you, Dakota. His name is Chandler Braddock and he's one of the best in the field. I'll call or email my father to talk to Chandler and send him our way. Is there room on the third floor?"

"Yes, we have three rooms on the other side of the hallway. He can have the room across from you," Dakota said.

"Thanks. It'll need to be altered for him, but I'll deal with it later."

"If you ask me before doing something and give me legitimate reasons for the request or change, I'll listen. I may not always agree, but I'll listen and consider. This"—Dakota waved a hand between them—"is all new to me. I'm used to having Edward and his wife here taking care of things."

"We'll figure a way through everything. I'll discuss things, I promise."

"Good. It'll prevent a lot of arguments."

Samuel chuckled and lifted his head when a soft knock interrupted them.

Dakota twisted and waved to Cecile to enter the office. "Hey, sweetie, you're done early. How did we do tonight?"

"Things were straightforward, no crazy tickets. We managed over fifteen thousand in sales and pretty decent in tips," she said as she handed over a blue zippered pouch and folder. "Tally list is on top as normal and double signed by Mal. Deposit is ready for the morning."

Samuel lifted an eyebrow at the number. "Is this normal?"

"Hmm, but it can vary due to the seasons and occupancy," Dakota said, looking through the folder at the report. "Sometimes it depends on what I'm serving. We'll do twice this amount and more during the main season which we consider May through September. The rest of the time we hope for good numbers to keep us going."

"Don't hurricanes come through those months as well?"

"They don't always curl in our direction," Dakota said.

"What if they do?"

"We keep a close eye out for the various weather reports. If needed, we follow procedures to protect everyone and everything. At times, we board up, cross the bridge and head beyond Pensacola with evacuation orders."

"Do you need anything else from me, boss?" Cecile asked.

"No, go on home and get some sleep. I'll see you tomorrow. Are all the others out?"

"Yup. The staff sanitized the kitchen and left after Malcolm's walk-through." She glanced at Samuel and back to Dakota.

"What is it?"

"Allan was hanging around to find you."

"Shit... What is he doing back here? I thought he was gone, Cecile," Dakota said.

"He showed me a handwritten note from you to welcome you back when he returned from wherever he went to. He never said a word about where he was other than a failed attempt to get through a college semester."

"A note? I never gave him a note."

"I'm sorry, Dakota, I should have verified it with you."

"No, no, don't worry about it."

"Do you want me to ask him to leave?"

"Not yet. Keep a close eye on him, though. I don't want him working without you. When you work, he works, and vice versa."

"Understood, boss. I'll keep him at tables near me and away from the kitchen. If he doesn't follow rules I'll tell him not to return for his next shift. Is there anything else?"

"We're finished for tonight. Go home, it's late. Get some sleep."

"Okay. Night, boys," Cecile said with a wave of her fingers as she left the office.

"Good night, Cecile. It was wonderful to meet you," Samuel called out.

Dakota rose again to return to the safe. Samuel spun in his chair and watched him enter a code and press a finger against the pad.

When the approval beep sounded, Dakota opened the heavy door.

"What's in there?" Samuel asked.

"The extra cash we have from closing the two registers. Anything private for the customers, who request we keep something in our safe. We have them sign a special form if they do to describe the item, include a photo if necessary, and sign and date. It protects them and the hotel. There are also some additional ledgers and copies of reports."

"More ledgers?"

"Yeah, how many should we have?"

"I don't know. Could I have those ledgers and reports? I would like Chandler to go through them."

"Sure. Whatever you want to do, I'm not the money man. I left it to Edward and Thomas." Dakota reached in farther and pulled out a thick expandable file. He held it out for Samuel to take.

"Thank you. I'll make sure Chandler knows the significance of these when he arrives. I'll lock them in this bottom drawer and keep the key with me,"

Samuel said as he turned and put it away in the drawer.

Dakota reset the lock and covered it with the painting. He tugged on the chair to spin Samuel back around. He braced his hands on the arms.

Samuel pulled back to meet the man's enigmatic gaze. "What..."

Dakota slid his fingers down Samuel's jaw and tilted it to capture his mouth. He played out the kiss, licking and teasing him. He stroked his tongue against Samuel's lower lip, asking for permission to enter. Samuel opened to the gentle request and Dakota took the kiss deeper. One of them moaned, the noise vibrating their lips. Tilting his head, Dakota continued to dive in to taste more. With his hand around Samuel's neck, he encouraged him to stand and pressed his ass against the desk. Moving his other hand to Samuel's neck, Dakota forced Samuel's knees apart and stepped between them. He continued the lick, nip and deep kiss.

Really shouldn't kiss him. Not again. Damn, this man can kiss.

Cold air wafted over his chest and he realized the man had opened his shirt. A thumb brushed over his nipple and he shivered at Dakota finding and touching one of his personal hot spots.

"Hmm, it seems these are sensitive," Dakota murmured. The quick break of their lips allowed them to gulp in several deep breaths.

"Please..."

Another plucking of Dakota's thumb on his nipple, circling it with a nail, and it puckered under the shirt. Goosebumps broke across his skin as Dakota touched him. The room spun. He faced the desk, bent over the edge, his ass pointed to the air.

"What the hell…?"

Dakota nipped at his neck. He shoved his erection against Samuel's ass. "Do you want this?"

Samuel pressed his hands on the desk and pushed back. "Get off me!"

"You've wanted this since we tumbled together upstairs."

"Not like this…"

"Tell me you haven't stayed half aroused all day." Dakota rolled his hips.

"Get off…"

Dakota strolled to the doorway. He braced a shoulder against the frame, dragged a hand through his hair, and shifted his cock.

Dropping back in the chair, gripping the arms, Samuel tried to remember how to breathe. Dakota pushed away from the door and returned to him. Samuel gripped the plastic handles until his knuckles turned white. The chef dropped to his knees and placed his head on Samuel's lap. Those talented hands clutched around his waist.

"What is…? Dakota?"

"Don't take my home from me. Don't take my restaurant away."

"I…I don't understand what you're doing. Dakota, please."

"I'm on my knees, pleading for everything I have in my life. This is all I ask," Dakota said, dropping all pretenses of arrogance and strength from his tone and attitude. He rubbed his cheek against Samuel's thighs.

"You don't need to do this. Please, get off your knees. There's no reason for you to behave this way." Samuel hovered his fingers over the soft hair, wanting to stroke the strands and comfort this man on the brink of falling apart.

Dakota lifted his head and stared up at Samuel. "This is all I have in my life. No family. No significant other. Nothing. The Charm is everything."

"Where's your family?"

"Chicago, but I don't see them. I haven't since I came out and took off for culinary school."

"What about Edward?"

"He was a father figure and friend, but now he's gone."

"Because of the sale…"

"Don't rip the rest of my life away. We can save this old building from failing. I'll do whatever I must to help save everything I love here." Those enigmatic sky blue eyes glistened with tears.

Unable to resist, Samuel cupped Dakota's face between his hands. He lifted the man toward him, placed a soft kiss on Dakota's lips. The man let out a tangled breath before he responded. Pulling back, but not releasing his grip, Samuel studied the handsome face.

"Sleep easy, my chef, and let me work. I'm not going to destroy the Charm or your restaurant. That isn't my intention. I need to figure out everything to help you protect what you created."

"Do you promise me?"

"I do."

"I'll hold you to it."

"I know. I wouldn't expect any less of you." Samuel released the man. "Sleep. You look exhausted."

A little unsteady, Dakota stood on his feet. He shifted his weight from one to the other. He shoved a hand in his pocket. "What about you? Are you staying down here?"

"I need to get a little further into all this paperwork so I'm staying put. I hope you have a good night," Samuel said.

Dakota lifted an eyebrow and nodded. He left the office.

Chapter Six

Shifting and rearranging the piles of papers several different times, Samuel realized he'd looked through them multiple times. His desk remained a disaster. He needed to create some type of sense from the chaos. Samuel searched for an office equipment and supply company online. He searched through various sections to study what he would need. Rising, he located a tape measure to evaluate a couple of walls in his office and the small office he would have Chandler use. Once he noted the measurements, he returned to the website. He chose necessary lateral cabinets, folders, labels, boards, and desk organizers. He couldn't believe these basic necessities were missing. After another search of the desk and empty supply closet, Samuel shook his head and added more supplies to his order. He created a new office account with the option to pay by invoice and set up the delivery.

After securing the numerous supplies, Samuel took a few more hours until he managed to make a decent enough dent in the various piles of paperwork. He placed them into smaller more structured groups, readying them for when all his supplies arrived and they could be moved to the appropriate folders and drawers.

When he glanced at one of the multiple clocks, he squinted and leaned closer. He double checked the time. He gasped at the sight of three fifteen. He groaned when he realized it was a.m. The same numbers were on all the screens. With that time yelling at him, he shut everything down, rose from the desk, and shut the door to the office to prevent anyone from disrupting all his work.

Even with the exhaustion pulling at him, he knew he wouldn't sleep. His insomnia plagued him whenever he was deep in paperwork of a new project. His mind filled, turning over the figures, sorting through the overload of information, and it wouldn't shut down.

Instead of heading upstairs, he slipped through the dark restaurant to the porch doors. He unlocked one of the doors, slid it open, and traversed outside. The humidity of the day lingered even into this late hour and foretold another humid day. Stretching his hands straight into the air, he elongated his spine, relishing in the pops and cricks as the knotted muscles released. He kicked off his shoes by the railing, rolled up his pants and jogged down the stairs. The sand was cool under his feet.

He slid and moved across the sand. Not used to walking in sand, he was a little unsteady from it and his exhaustion. He looked around at the quiet, dark beauty of the beach. Plopping his ass down in the sand, he dismissed the idea of the damage to his pants, and stuck his legs out.

After a flex of his feet, he drew his knees up and wrapped his arms around them. He stared out across the beautiful dark water, saw the white foam curls as the waves rolled in and broke across the sand. He closed his eyes as he listened to the soothing natural music.

Moving, he leaned back on his elbows, watched the beautiful moon hanging over the dark water, lighting the waves in the soft glow. There was no breeze other than what the ocean created.

It was perfect.

Why was this beach empty? Why was this beautiful old home on the edge of closing? Why did no one wish to return to this peaceful retreat? The damaging oil had been removed, the beaches cleaned – the water was clear and there wasn't anyone enjoying this place.

There were mysteries within all the figures and the hotel itself. He needed to keep working, searching, and locating both the questions and answers. In spite of his father's insistence, he needed to find something he could do to save and revitalize both the Charm and this town which relied upon it.

Losing all track of time as he observed the waves, he contemplated the moon meandering through the sky in the endless, eternal cycle. Yawning, he stretched his arms and rubbed his neck. There was something restful about the sea.

Hoping he could fall asleep for at least a couple of hours, Samuel rolled back to his feet. As he headed back, he brushed the cool sand off his clothes. Amused at how the finest dry sand clung to the cloth, he jumped a few times to knock the last of it off. When he stepped on the porch, he leaned down and swept his feet as clean as he could. He slid his feet back in the loafers, grimacing at the feel, and went back inside. He locked the door.

This time, he lightly climbed the stairs to the third floor. He headed down the hall to his corner room.

Before he could open his door, he heard the click of another lock. He turned to see Dakota's door open. The man stepped out in a different outfit with jogging shoes. A morning scruff of beard darkened his jaw. The jaw he'd held between his hands. Those full lips he'd kissed.

"Hey there," Samuel said as he turned to lean on the frame.

Dakota looked up in sleepy surprise. "Hey."

"Did you sleep well?"

"I got a few hours."

"What are you doing up?" Samuel asked on the edge of another yawn.

"I'm heading out. Are you just now going to bed?"

"I'm having a bit of insomnia."

"That sucks."

"Big time."

"Does it happen a lot?"

"On and off since I left college and started full-time at my family's company. If I'm under more stress, like a major solo project, the damn disorder hits me harder. I have pills, but I hate taking them."

"So by being down here and on a new job, you can't sleep. Where were you if not in your office?"

Samuel yawned with a brief nod. "I decided to sit outside on the beach for a couple of hours and listened to the waves."

"They're a good natural soother."

"Yeah, I never knew how peaceful and beautiful the ocean could be at night. I adored sitting there and doing nothing but watch the rolling waves. One would have no idea about all the problems or issues while sitting there."

Dakota looked away. "It was peaceful for the longest time, the coast a picture of perfection."

"Sorry. I didn't mean to bring up the bad stuff or memories."

"Doesn't matter, I try not to dwell on it. I need to get going."

"Where are you going?"

"I'm heading around town to take care of business, going for a run, and finishing with a swim. It's something I do every morning to counteract all the calories I inhale in the kitchen," Dakota said. "Do I need your permission now to leave the hotel?"

Samuel straightened and stepped over. "Why are you so damn harsh to me? You were on your knees and pleading with me. Now your attitude is all piss and vinegar. What the hell is with this bipolar attack upon me?"

"You're trying to take away my home and my business."

"Don't start this up again, please. I thought we went over this last night. I'm not taking away anything. My family purchased this place to help it survive and thrive. Nothing will be destroyed."

"Unless you figure out it isn't worth keeping the doors opened."

"I gave you my word I wouldn't close or destroy the Charm. I believe in my word and promise when I offer it."

"I don't know if I should trust you."

"That is something you must figure out and I can't help you. I say again, nothing will happen to the Charm while I'm here. I haven't figured anything yet. I need your help to make these decisions. You know this place better. I need to know what you do and how this place runs to get an accurate picture of the business." Samuel dragged a hand down his face and scratched at his neck. He let out a long frustrated breath. "Everything you do or tell me will influence the decision. It'll give me more information so I can figure out what's happening."

"Or use it against me."

With another grumble, Samuel tilted his head and looked up at him. "Are you always this distrustful of everyone you meet? Do you snap at someone you kiss the day before?"

Straightening, Dakota narrowed his gaze.

"Hell…" Samuel muttered as he stepped in, wrapped a hand around the man's neck, and yanked him down. He let his lips linger across the bristled jaw before he went along his slanted cheekbone. He moved his fingers until they teased the short hairs at the base of Dakota's skull. He lifted on his toes to nuzzle the pale evening growth.

He used his fingers to tilt Dakota's head down as he lifted to press their lips together in a warm, searching kiss. After their lips met, brushed, then separated, he was stunned when Dakota opened his lips to invite him to go deeper instead of pushing him away. The kiss was slower and more thorough.

Dakota wrapped his arms around Samuel. He kissed Samuel as his grip tightened around him. Dakota took over the kiss by leaning back. He slanted his head and captured Samuel's lips in another harder kiss. He shoved his thigh between Samuel's legs and lifted him higher. He pressed Samuel against the nearest wall, his muscled leg snug between Samuel's, until their hips slotted together.

Samuel moaned against Dakota's mouth. He readjusted his hold on Dakota's shoulders as Dakota's leg nudged his cock.

Dakota stepped back, breaking the kiss, and let Samuel drop back on his feet. He gave him another peck on his lips then stroked his fingers down Samuel's cheek. Moving away to the stairs, he glanced over his shoulder. "Try and get some sleep."

Samuel opened his mouth to say something, but closed it. He tried again. "Can you tell me what type of business you're doing downtown?"

"It's business for the restaurant, typical stuff for me. No need to worry about it," the chef said and disappeared around the corner.

Rubbing a hand over his swollen lips, Samuel stared at the empty stairwell. *Damn, the chef is one helluva kisser, but insufferable for leaving me high and with a freaking boner.* He fumbled with the key in the lock.

Grumbling but too exhausted to follow the man, Samuel entered the cool dark room, kicked the door shut, stripped his clothes, and face planted on the bed. His erect cock pressed and rubbed against the sheets. It craved the friction to bring release.

Flipping on his back, Samuel reached under his pillow for lube. He squeezed a pile in his palm. He wrapped his hand around his cock and gave himself a long pull and twist. He knew exactly what he needed to come. Dakota brought him damn close and left him alone.

"Damn, Chef, I want your lips wrapped around me," he said as he moved his fist faster. His balls pulled up and he called out Dakota's name as ropes of cum spurted from the slit, covering his hand and belly. He continued to masturbate until his balls emptied and his cock softened.

Draping his other arm over his face, Samuel groaned as he came down from the release. There was no way he could keep things platonic. Not with Dakota starring in his masturbation fantasies. This wasn't going to end well.

Rolling over, he grabbed his T-shirt and used it to wipe off his hand, belly, and cock. Tossing it away, he shifted back on his side. Wrapping his arms around the pillow, he shoved his face into the softness and groaned in this simple pleasure. Thanks to the hard release, he fell fast asleep with Dakota haunting his dreams.

Chapter Seven

After four days of everything and everyone acting exactly the same, Samuel was ready to scream, stomp, and holler. He hated how no one stepped out of their way to lend him a hand or offer any type of help. Leaning back in the chair, Samuel shoved his hands through his hair and banged a hand on the desk.

Every morning after a soothing walk on the beach, sometimes minutes after Samuel entered his room, Dakota—his partner and his nemesis—left his room to disappear on his mysterious errands. Falling asleep was inevitable, but Dakota returned a couple of hours later to shower and sleep. By the time Samuel dressed to head downstairs, he often caught a glimpse of Dakota leaving ahead of him. Dakota would be dressed in another outfit, his hair damp, his face shaved, and acting like nothing had happened. Since Dakota left in khaki shorts and a nice shirt every morning first thing, Samuel wondered where he stashed his running and swimming shorts. Part of him wanted to follow and watch the lean figure swim in a pair of shorts or even better a Speedo. Oh yeah, he would enjoy seeing Dakota's body and cock captured in a tiny Speedo.

"What the hell is he doing every morning that requires a pre-dawn trip? Crazy man goes for a freaking run and a morning dunk in the ocean. No one should be so damn committed to fitness crap outside a decent gym," Samuel muttered to the empty office. He picked up a pen and tapped it with no rhythm against the desk. "Coffee, figuring out this newest mystery requires coffee."

Pushing up from the chair, Samuel shoved hands in the pockets of his pressed khakis and wandered toward the kitchen, but found it empty and quiet.

"Odd."

The scent of fresh coffee and…bacon lingered.

Sniffing, Samuel grinned. "I could do with a few strips of crisped pork fat." He followed the aromas which led him to the restaurant. He heard voices from within the room and stood next to the open doorway.

Along one wall was a table filled with a simple buffet of breakfast foods and two containers of coffee with all the fixings next to it. Several tables were pushed together and it appeared most of the employees were gathered around it, eating, talking or listening. Dakota was at one end with Elise next to him. This meeting of some sort was yet another thing no one had invited him to attend. They kept him apart, on the outside of their group, and out of the picture until they knew what to do with him or what he would decide about the Charm.

"I spoke with Jude. He'll send over magnolia and gardenia blossoms. I asked for purple lilacs, but they were a little expensive. The bride is a southern girl and had magnolia and gardenia blossoms in her wedding along with the purple and white lilacs. She's allergic to roses and lilies," Elise said as she checked the notes.

"Why are they staying here?" Malcolm asked.

"The couple spent their first intimate weekend here three years ago and he proposed to her last year on the deck. He's surprising her for the honeymoon by taking her here for a week and they'll go somewhere else for another week."

"Aww, that's sweet of him. Why can't I find a guy like that?" Mal asked.

"Because you're chained to the kitchen and don't go outside," one of the other kitchen helpers said with a snort.

Others snickered around them as Mal dropped his head on his arms and banged his forehead a few times. "Thanks, Dorian, love you too, kid," Mal said to the teasing kid.

"More than welcome to keep you on the straight and narrow path," Dorian said.

Glenn reached out and popped Dorian on the back of his head with the flat of his hand. "Knock it off, kid."

"He started it..."

Glenn lifted his hand and Dorian clamped his mouth shut.

"Okay. Back to the meeting, boys," Elise said.

"What else is done for a honeymooning couple?" Samuel asked as he entered the room and headed straight to the coffee brewers. He grabbed a mug from the pile and filled his cup with the dark fragrant brew. He propped against the table, sipped from the mug, and stared at all of them. "Other than flowers in the room, I mean."

"Samuel, I didn't know you wanted to join our little meeting this morning," Dakota said.

"As the new co-owner and representing Ashford Hotels, I believe I should be included in all meetings. Since all approvals for potential business items must be passed on my desk for attention, signature, and payment, I should know what is happening," Samuel said.

Dakota lifted an eyebrow and glanced around the table. He returned his gaze to meet Samuel's stare. "When did this happen?"

"A recent change in procedure I put into place. Since we haven't spoken in some time like we planned, I couldn't pass it along. I wrote a detailed memo and left it on your desk."

"You left a memo on my desk."

"Hmm, it was a detailed one. I was quite fond of the work. It wasn't the only one. I left multiple ones, at least one a day, to update you."

"I don't like memos."

"You should take time to speak with me. I'm sure it would save a lot of unnecessary memos and wasted paper." Lifting the mug, Samuel sipped the coffee, kept his gaze upon Dakota over the edge.

The other employees all shifted in their chairs and mumbled under their breaths as Dakota and Samuel argued.

"This meeting is done. Everyone, grab your dishes and get back to work. Elise, do whatever you need to make our honeymooners comfortable and happy. I'll approve everything you need," Dakota said, not taking his attention from Samuel.

Elise glanced at Samuel and Dakota before she gathered her paperwork together. "Thanks, boss. See you two later."

"Have a good day, Elise. Perhaps we can talk later about what could be done further to accommodate specific clients so I can get a feel of how we treat their stay with us," Samuel said as he set his coffee on the table.

"Sure. That sounds like a good idea, Samuel, I wouldn't want you to be lost and kept out of the loop," Elise said with a glare at Dakota, who shrugged a shoulder.

"Thanks, Elise, I appreciate it. It isn't fun being the new guy, but I hope we can get over all the humps and issues together. The problem is the staff will follow Dakota's cues and behavior since he's senior management." Samuel glanced to Dakota to make sure the man was listening. "If he doesn't give me the time of day, neither will they. I'm sorry, but the situation fucking sucks and I want to find ways to remedy the issue so the wall between all of us disappears. I'm not looking to remove positions or fire anyone. It's not in my plans to take away anyone's position, but if no one helps me I can't do my job to help save the Charm from foreclosure," Samuel said.

Elise glared again at Dakota. "Listen to the New Yorker and stop being an ass," she said before she left for the front desk area.

Dakota's eyes widened at the smart retort from her.

Samuel returned to the breakfast buffet to fill a plate. He carried it to the table and sat down with deliberate motions. "I hope you don't mind if I get something to eat. I'm starving."

"You can help yourself, as always," Dakota said with a wave of his hand. "We do this meeting about once a week to catch up about all the guests and restaurant business. It's easier to do it in the morning over breakfast before the guests become active."

Samuel ate the meal, delicious as always considering who had cooked the darn stuff. "I didn't know anything about this until I heard all the voices. I was searching for coffee."

"Sorry. Thought I mentioned something to Malcolm to invite you," Dakota said.

"No, you didn't! Don't even thing about blaming your shit on me, Dakota," Malcolm called as he entered the room to begin breaking down the buffet.

"Pain in the ass," Dakota muttered.

"But he's an honest fella," Samuel said, "unlike someone else sitting at this table."

Dakota leaned forward. "Do you have a problem with me?"

"I don't know what my issue is with you. You run so damn hot and cold around me, I find myself going in circles figuring out how to handle you. Once I think we're on a good start, you throw a freaking roadblock in my path and we're back to square one. I'm trying to do what is best for the Charm. How can I if we don't cooperate? We need to work together during this integration into the Ashford chain. I've asked and requested multiple times."

"I don't work with someone who is threatening to close down my home, my life, because he isn't happy about something."

"Is that all you heard from the entire conversation? I thought we went through all those concerns with some assertions I'm not closing anything."

"It's a little damn important to me. Unlike you, I don't have a rich mommy and daddy to run home to and support me."

"My family doesn't support me. I work for the hotel chain and earn every damn dollar I am paid, and have done since I entered at the bottom of the corporation." Samuel pushed away the plate, having lost his appetite during the argument. Not even the perfect crisp slices of pork fat, the manna from heaven known as bacon, could tempt him. He grabbed his mug, filled it once again, and headed to the door.

"Are you walking away when things don't go your way?"

"No. I'm walking away before I jump the table and bitch slap you for being an asshole," Samuel shot back and left the room.

"Boo-yah, you go, Yankee," Malcolm said to Samuel's back. He'd entered again for another round of clean-up. "I can't believe you, Dakota."

"Shut it, Mal," Dakota said.

"No, you shut it." Mal pointed a finger at him. "This is your fault. Every fucked up thing happening right now is due to you and your damn attitude."

"Are you done?"

"Hell, fucking no! You're the reason for all the damn tension around here. Figure it out. You have one option left, buddy."

"Which is?"

"You need to stop being an ass, suck it up, and fix it," Mal said.

"That's three options."

"Don't be picky," Mal said, finishing the clean-up as he snapped at his boss. He lifted the last of the trays and walked away.

Dakota leaned back in the chair and thrummed his fingers on the table.

Chapter Eight

As the day pushed closer to lunch, Samuel stayed in the back office fuming over this morning. How could the man be so damn obtuse?

The knock on the door brought his head up with a growl. "What?" he asked before he saw Elise standing in the doorway. "Sorry, shit, I'm sorry, Elise. I didn't mean to snap."

"Not a problem. Sorry for the interruption, sir, but the delivery folks from the supply company are here with your new cabinets and other items," Elise said.

"Yes, good timing on their part. I need those moved in," Samuel said as he looked around the cluttered offices. "Four will go along that wall and the other two in the smaller office."

"Fellas, come on in and take a look at what we're working with in here. I think it's going to be kinda tight," Elise said over her shoulder.

Two burly fellas in uniforms of the supply company stepped into the room.

"Please excuse the clutter, but I haven't the room to place anything and prepare for your arrival," Samuel said as he stepped forward and held out his hand. "Hello, I'm Samuel Ashford."

"I'm Paul. This is my buddy, Ray. We've seen worse places. Where do you want the lateral cabinets?" the dark-haired Paul said as he shook Samuel's hand.

The quiet Hispanic fellow behind him nodded and shook hands.

Dakota appeared in the doorway. "What's going on in here?"

Samuel grumbled and dragged a hand through his hair. "I ordered filing cabinets and supplies to get organization into this place. If you don't mind, I need to get everything moved around so I can begin to clean things."

"Do you need a hand in moving things?" Dakota offered.

"Aren't you needed in the kitchen?"

"Mal has it covered. How about you move all those piles across the hall into my office to make room? You can organize and carry over what you need."

Samuel looked around the floor and Dakota. "Sounds like a good idea. You won't be able to use your office for the next day or so."

Dakota shrugged. "No problem. I can get what I need and carry it to the kitchen or my room."

"Thank you," Samuel said.

"Welcome. Let's get this show moving," Dakota said.

"Sounds like a plan," Paul said. He and his partner helped create a line from Samuel's office and into Dakota's room.

When other employees saw what was happening, they joined in the line. Working together with Samuel gathering the various piles and passing them to the helpers to move everything across the hall, the necessary space became cleared with ease.

"Great. Thank you, everyone," Samuel called out. "Okay, could you please move the two lateral cabinets into the back room on the one wall?"

"Sure. We'll unpack and roll them in," Paul said with a nod to his partner before they walked away.

"I've been telling Edward for years he needed a better filing system than boxes of paperwork stashed away," Dakota said.

"Boxes? There are more boxes stashed away."

"You didn't find the other boxes he put in the closet."

"I saw what was all over the floor and desk. There's more in the closet?" Samuel asked, drawing out the last question.

Dakota moved to the closet, hidden by one of the stacks of boxes, and opened it to reveal the columns of white labeled storage boxes.

"Oh. My. God." Samuel's jaw dropped.

"I think it goes about four rows deep. I never dared pull anything out of this place for fear it would collapse on me."

"Oh. My. God." Samuel lifted on his toes and looked around the inside of the closet. "I had no idea." He gulped at the project ahead of him. "I may need another cabinet."

"He wasn't sure what he should shred, toss, retire…or what to keep. So he kept everything and anything dealing with the hotel."

"How long?"

"I think around twenty years, perhaps longer, but I'm not sure. The time is a give or take. I do know he continued adding boxes on top of the ones from the previous owner and when he purchased the Charm."

Samuel thudded his forehead against the door. "Close. Close it, please, before I hyperventilate."

Dakota closed the door and moved to Samuel's side. He rubbed his hand over Samuel's drooped shoulders to soothe him.

"I had no idea. I don't..." Samuel gulped. "I don't know if I can do this. It's so much..."

"Just take it one step at a time. Go with the current stuff, which is everything outside this closet. I think it covers the last five years."

"Five? Five years of paperwork we shifted around?"

Dakota nodded.

Samuel whimpered in fear of what was ahead of him. "I need Chandler to get his ass down here. He knows his shit when it comes to numbers. I gotta look into getting him down here."

"Hopefully, he can help you," Dakota said. "I'm sorry there is such a mess in here. Not to mention, we haven't gone near the restaurant side. I'm sure there are numerous troubles within there."

"At least you have cabinets. You do use them, right?"

"Umm. I have a little bit of order in them."

Samuel whimpered.

"I know. I know." Dakota held up his hands and returned one hand to Samuel's shoulder. "Damn, you have some massive knots in there." He moved around Samuel and began to dig his fingers into the muscles.

Samuel moaned in pure pleasure, lowered his head to give Dakota more access. "Oh man, that feels good." As the delightful massage continued, Samuel weakened in his anger against Dakota, but only for this precious brief moment. He leaned back against the taller man and sighed.

Dakota leaned down and brushed his lips against Samuel's in a light, brief kiss.

Samuel's eyes popped open as he stared at the man. *What the hell is going on with him?* This was a total change from this morning. Before he could turn and deepen the kiss, the noises of the movers made them jump apart. They separated farther before the two men entered and rolled the cabinet between them.

"Umm. Hey. Over this way, fellas," Samuel said, clearing his throat.

"I'll stop back in later to see if you need a hand," Dakota said after the movers stepped past him.

"Uhh. Thanks. Thanks, Dakota, I appreciate all of the help to get this moved around." Samuel waved a hand and moved it over his mouth.

"No problem. Do you want some lunch? How about you guys?" Dakota moved to the door.

Paul glanced at his partner, who shrugged and nodded. "That sounds great. Whatever you have available would be good. We'll eat after we finish."

"Same here," Samuel said. "Thanks again."

"Not a problem, I'll have everything ready," Dakota said and left the office.

Clearing his throat again, Samuel helped them maneuver the first of several cabinets into their places.

Dakota listened to him. Holy shit, he was surprised. This friendly Dakota was an interesting turn to things between them. He wondered how long it would last.

Chapter Nine

Three days had passed by the time that Samuel had moved all the various boxes back into his office area. He needed to figure out how to sort and combine everything he found in the closet with the stuff lying around the offices. He dreaded opening the closet again. Even though Dakota started being friendly, Samuel didn't want to give him a reason to become pissed. To keep the peace, he wouldn't leave anything lying around Dakota's space or confront him. So what if it meant him playing chicken for a bit. He could handle being a chicken to keep the atmosphere pleasant.

Instead, he brought everything back to his office and kept his work out of Dakota's space. He began the tedious work of laying out the various piles of corresponding paperwork to begin some kind of filing system. He sat on the floor, surrounded by stacks of boxes, binders, papers, hanging and manila folders, and labels with pens and pencils strewn about him.

True to his word and surprising the hell out of Samuel, Dakota made sure he was eating by dropping off plates of food and full pitchers of the delicious sun tea. The man even offered to help, but backed off when Samuel didn't accept.

Of course, neither mentioned the kisses or the growing tension between them. There was no way he would bring it up and spark another argument. He was tired of constantly trying to protect or support his stance and decisions both to Dakota and, at times, his own father. He didn't want to give up on the Charm, not until he'd learned all the intricate secrets within the scattered paperwork and numbers.

Exhausted by the work, Samuel rubbed against his tired, burning eyes. He tugged off the simple tortoiseshell reading glasses he needed for details.

"That's it, I've had enough," he muttered to no one.

Knowing he'd barely made a dent into the files, Samuel rolled his head back and forth. He pushed himself to his feet, pressed hands against his lower back, and stretched and popped his vertebrae.

Stepping out of the office, Samuel didn't hear the usual noise which accompanied the busy kitchen. He glanced at his watch — it was after ten in the evening. He groaned, shoved a hand through his hair. As he had the first night he'd been here, he needed to get out and clear his mind. He walked through the empty restaurant to the wall of doors. He opened one, stepped outside, and lifted his face to the gentle breeze and soft moonlight. Immediately, under the lull of the waves and moon, he felt his body begin to relax.

He kicked off his shoes and headed down the stairs. Within moments, his feet sank into the soft sand, still retaining some warmth of the earlier sun but cooling fast. The moon lit his way down to the water's edge as the waves broke across the damp sand in the low tide.

He dropped down on the dry sand at the delineated line drawn over ancient times and endless waves.

Reclining on the sand, he stretched out his legs, wiggled his feet in the cooler wetter sand, and leaned on his elbows. He studied the beautiful moon-tipped waves as they rolled and crashed onto land before returning to the dark ocean. The sound was nature at her finest.

"You're going to ruin those nice chinos by sitting in the sand," someone said in a soft voice behind him.

Samuel tilted his head to see a tall figure standing over him. The moon lit Dakota with the same pearly light—and damn if the man didn't look even more handsome.

"It's dry sand. It'll brush off," Samuel said.

"You need different clothes to relax and chill out while you're down here," Dakota said as he plopped down on the sand and stretched out his long legs, bared underneath the board shorts. "Same with your loafers, they don't belong on the beach."

"I never planned on having time to relax or lay out under the sun so I didn't bring those outfits."

"Don't want to take a swim in the ocean?"

"Is it safe?"

Dakota turned to him, lifted an eyebrow. "Yeah. I swim in it every morning after a run up and down the beach. Why do you ask?"

"I thought the ocean would be damaged from the oil spill."

"Are you talking about the Horizon accident?"

Samuel nodded.

Dakota groaned and shook his head. "This is why we're having trouble getting people to visit us." He pinched the bridge of his nose and sighed.

"Sorry, I didn't mean to…"

"No. No. It's something we need to figure out how to get the message to potential visitors at how everything is safe. There isn't any damage lingering in our area. We were cleared by the oil people and the environmentalists."

"How bad was it down here?"

Dakota picked up a handful of sand and watched as it sifted back to the beach. He did it multiple times as if he used the motion to think about his answer. "After it first happened, there was dread all over the Gulf. As the damn thing spilled barrels and they couldn't cap it off, we felt helpless."

"But it didn't come this far over."

"As more time passed, it became larger and factored in the winds, tides and currents. Multiple blobs appeared across our beaches."

Samuel leaned his shoulder against Dakota's arm, felt the muscles bunch and flex against his skin. He lowered his head to Dakota's shoulder to offer quiet comfort.

"Instead of all the boats going off to make their daily catches, they were equipped with those yellow floating things to catch and control the oil. Every morning, they sifted and gathered the horrible oil. The clean-up took months, years in some areas to make things better, not perfect, but better."

"All the time, you had no tourists at the Charm."

"We gave rooms to volunteer clean-up groups, environmentalists, and some of the oil company folks. Anyone who was doing work and needed a place to stay, we welcomed them here."

"How much were they charged?"

"I think Edward charged them about a hundred a week. Which isn't much, but they were here to help."

"Did you get help from the company and FEMA?"

"We put in our requests."

"Ugh. I wonder if the reply is somewhere in the mess."

"Knowing Edward, probably," Dakota said with a lopsided smile.

"Guess I better move that statement or report better to the top of my list of things to find," Samuel said with a groan and flopped flat on his back.

The sand shifted around him and the moonlight darkened when Dakota braced a hand on his far side to lean over him. The bare minimum silver light highlighted Dakota's golden-tipped hair as his body hovered over Samuel.

Samuel looked up at him, blinked in a slow way. "Why are you being so..."

"You mean why I'm different from the morning you snapped at me after the meeting."

Dakota shrugged. "I listened to what you told me. I had some additional kicks to my stubborn ass after you left. Either I stop being such an ass to you or the only change I do is to my attitude."

"Is this because others told you to get your head out of your ass?"

"I agreed with them and some of the suggestions. The Charm needs to change, be enhanced, or I will lose her and my home."

"You know I'm here to help."

"You're the only one who can help us or destroy us."

"I don't destroy..."

"Ssh, I didn't mean it like that," Dakota soothed, resting sandy fingers on Samuel's lips.

"I'm trying to save what you love, but make it better. I've been fighting with my father to let me continue the work. If he gets his way, the Charm would close, but not the restaurant. You still own the Delights."

"But the Charm would be empty and shut down to visitors."

"Exactly and I'm trying to make him see given time I can figure out the solution beneficial to both places."

"Does he want to give up on the Charm?"

"He isn't sure if there would be a monetary value to the chain if we put in all of this capital into the project."

"Sounds like a lot of mumbo jumbo executive talk I don't understand."

"There are times I don't either, but I fought his decision. My mother is supporting me. She wants a series of unique hotels to reflect the beauty and culture of various areas. We want to keep it, but make things a little more cost efficient."

Dakota lowered his forehead touching Samuel's with a light touch. "I have no idea what you're talking about when it comes to all these numbers. I know the basics to purchase and cook the food according to menu prices and revenues. Other than that, I have no idea about the details."

"Sorry, didn't mean to go on like that."

"No. No. It's charming how you do it." Dakota lifted his head and stared down into Samuel's gaze. "You're adorable and cute when you get stuck on a subject you're either protesting or saving."

"Cute? I'm not cute."

"You're cute, don't argue."

"I'm damn determined in what I want. I don't want you to lose everything you work for and I'm willing to fight."

"I don't want to lose my home either," Dakota said and moved his gaze to take in the looming structure behind them. "Everything I've done the last fifteen years is wrapped in the Charm. I moved from restaurant to restaurant, learning my way, working my way up once I left school, but the Delights. This is my baby, my design, my recipes and my heart." He tilted his head back down.

Amazed, Samuel caught a glimpse of a glistening tears forming at the corners of Dakota's eyes. "Hey there, please, don't be sad."

"I don't know how we'll save the old place. So much has happened and I don't know if we can come back."

"We will. We're going to save her. I promise we'll make her stronger and better. Just like you're home after all those hurricanes and the oil spill. She'll still stand here."

Dakota met his gaze and drew a finger down Samuel's cheekbone.

Samuel pulled in his lower lip and chewed it.

"Hey...stop that," Dakota whispered, not much louder than the sound of the sea. He leaned down, brushed their lips together, before pulling back then deepening the kiss.

Samuel let his fingers tangle in Dakota's hair as he responded to the kiss. He stretched his legs out on the cool sand, his heels digging deeper, as he arched against Dakota's harder frame.

Damn the man can kiss!

Dakota lifted his head, grinned, then moved his hands to crumple Samuel's shirt. He tugged it away from the waistband, opened the buttons, licked along the collarbone, and nuzzled the shallow between them. At Samuel's soft moan of encouragement, he kissed a path exposed by the shirt. He nudged the cloth out of his way when he needed. He circled his tongue around one nipple and bit down with a light firm touch.

"Oh shit, yeah," Samuel said.

"Are you gonna come from me licking your nipples?"

"I could."

"It would be hot, but there is something else I want to do before you blow your load." Dakota moved his mouth around the pectorals before following the trail of brunet hair. "Hmm, I like a little body hair." He brushed his chin against some of the swirls.

"What...what are you doing?"

"Helping you relax," Dakota said as he lowered his attention. He licked along the edge of the waistband, dipping his tongue behind the cloth. He blew along the damp line he'd kissed and marked.

Samuel groaned as his body shuddered. "You can't... We can't..."

"Why not? It's a perfectly healthy thing to give a good blow job," Dakota said while he was busy with the button and zipper. He scooped inside and found another barrier. "Briefs? Really?"

"We don't know each other well enough to do this. I don't like swinging free when I wear wool trousers. It's a damn habit."

"One we'll have to break you out of while you're down here. I'll make sure to offer lots of encouragement."

"You're not listening, we shouldn't do this." Samuel placed his fingers over Dakota's busy hands before Dakota could pull his cock and balls free of the tight cloth.

"My hand is wrapped around your cock and you want to stop this. Do you want me to stop?"

Licking his lips, Samuel closed his eyes as Dakota circled a finger under the edge of his dark cockhead.

"Give us this moment under the moonlight, Samuel. It's a good way to learn how to relax." Dakota blew against the moist head of Samuel's cock when it emerged from behind the cotton cloth.

Samuel moaned. He tried to grip onto something, but the sand sifted.

"Such a pretty cock too. Look, your body wants this. I found some lovely drops ready for me to lick," Dakota said as he kept his gaze on Samuel while he licked across the slit with the flat of his tongue, capturing those precious droplets of pre-cum. He smacked his lips together and grinned. "Yum."

"You're crazy… This is crazy."

"But feels damn good," Dakota said before he opened his mouth and took Samuel's cock in his mouth. He swirled his tongue around the flared edge of the head, his hand wrapped around the base. Keeping tight suction, he bobbed his head, slicking the cock, his tongue playing against the thick blood vessels. Lifting up, he played along where the head and shaft met, licking droplets from the slit. Dakota squeezed and stroked Samuel's cock. He slipped his fingers under the soft sack of balls, fiddled with the guiche and the perineum.

"Sonofa…" Samuel let out on a groan as his hips bucked against Dakota when the man deep-throated and swallowed him. *It's been so long since anyone gave me a decent blow job.* "I can't…"

"Let go…" Dakota said as he squeezed and jacked as he swallowed him again.

With a strangled cry, Samuel unloaded his cum deep in Dakota's mouth. He heard the man swallow his cum, not letting any spill out. As he tried to figure out his breathing, he lowered his hips to the sand. One arm dropped over his face.

Dakota put his cock and balls in his briefs and closed his pants. He kissed back up Samuel's torso, swirling his tongue around the belly button, before he lowered the shirt. He didn't bother to tuck it back in place. He sat next to Samuel's hip, one knee raised.

Samuel touched Dakota's thigh, but when he went to find the erection, Dakota stopped him.

"Nope, not tonight," Dakota said.

"Don't you want...?"

"Nope." Dakota leaned forward and kissed him. "Just wanted to know what you tasted like."

"And..."

"You're delicious." Dakota gave him a deeper kiss.

Sliding his fingers into Dakota's hair, Samuel opened to the kiss as another moan escaped and ended in a cry of surprise. This one came from Samuel when he felt the cool ocean waves wash over his feet and ankles, dampening the khakis against his skin.

"Whoa... Whoa... Getting wet here," Samuel said as he pushed back Dakota.

"What? You're ready to cum again." Dakota wiggled against Samuel's hand to lower for another kiss.

"Umm. No. I'm talking about the tide coming in." Samuel scrambled away, and sat up to bring his feet away from the water's edge. "Oh man, I like these pants too."

Dakota turned to sit and study the ocean. "Hmm, looks like the evening high tide is coming in." He watched Samuel tug the wet trousers away from his lower legs. "You do need to pick up some shorts and T-shirts."

"Don't have the time to be concerned about my wardrobe. Shit...I need to get out of these and get them rinsed." Samuel pushed to his feet.

"What about..."

Samuel glanced down at him. "I'll see you tomorrow. Umm...thank..."

Dakota held up a hand. "Don't thank me, not for this. I've enjoyed the night too much. I'll see you in the morning."

With a swallow, Samuel turned and almost raced away. He was grateful for the ocean disturbing things. His body dragged through the wringer from the blow job. He had no idea what was happening between them. Well, shit, he knew it was sexual tension released thanks to the orgasm, but to roll around in the sand with the guy and have sex? Full out, woo-hoo, rock the bed kind of sex with the man he's argued with since he arrived. How could he think about falling in to bed with the man?

There was the blow job. Shit... Had a simple blow tossed his marbles out of whack? It had been a few months — shit, no, almost a year, since he'd had a partner.

So confused, Samuel grabbed his loafers and went inside the old house. He knew that it would be a long time before he would fall asleep, his mind tangled with feelings, nerves, and arousal.

Chapter Ten

Exhausted and restless after two nights of little sleep and long days of mind-numbing work, Samuel ran his hands over his face. He wasn't much deeper into the various piles of paperwork. He desperately needed Chandler's brain and expertise on this dive into the reams of paper strewn across the office. He reached for his laptop and tapped out another desperate plea to his father to send Chandler down to Florida. There were too many questions and issues which he didn't know about, but Chandler probably would within minutes. There was too much interconnecting information sent electronically or via delivery. He needed him in person to help see the patterns and connections. He hit send on the email and lifted the cool cup of coffee.

"Hey, boss. I got something for you," Elise called out in a friendly tone.

"Is it an automatic scanner and reader to tell me what's going on across these papers?" Samuel asked with a grin.

Elise chuckled and shook her head.

"Rats. I tried. Umm, do you know a decent IT person who can help us order new computers and a server?"

"Are we getting new computers and a server? One for the front desk too. Please? Please?" Elise bounced on her toes.

Samuel chuckled. "Yes. Do you know someone?"

"Hmm. You'll want to talk to Beau Courtenay. He's the local IT guru of this area, knows everything and anything about that kind of electronics."

"Do you have his number?"

Elise nodded and rattled off a local phone number.

"Whoa. Whoa. Wait a minute," Samuel said and scrambled for a pad and pen. "Say it one more time and his name."

Elise chuckled. "Beau Courtenay. Courtenay Tech," she said and spelled out the last name before she gave him the phone number, a website, and an email address.

"Great. Thank you. I'll give him a call and see what he recommends," Samuel said as he scribbled everything down. "You said you had something for me."

Elise leaned back, grabbed something, then plopped two bags on the ground in front of him. "A belated welcome gift from everyone at the Charm, boss."

"It's a welcome gift for me? Why? I mean..." Samuel blinked as he studied the bags. "You didn't have to do this for me."

"Dakota insisted we all make you feel welcome and thank you for saving our home. He suggested a few things and I went out with someone else."

"What did he suggest? You get me a one-way flight ticket back to New York? Only you put it inside multiple boxes and lots of paper?"

Elise chuckled and shook her head. "Is he still being a pain in the ass?"

"No, he isn't, but we have our moments," Samuel said as he plucked at one of the bags.

Elise tipped over one bag. "He suggested we pick you up some southern-styled clothes. A couple of pairs of sandals, some board shorts for swimming, others for day-to-day stuff, and some lighter weight shirts. It's mostly casual wear, which you don't seem to have packed for your stay."

Samuel's eyes widened as the clothes tumbled out from the bag. "He mentioned... But I didn't think he would..." He swallowed hard.

"Do you like the choices? I can give you the receipts or exchange anything."

"I umm... How did you know my sizes?"

Elise grinned. "I peeked into your dresser drawers and closets."

"Oh, nice one."

Elise chuckled and walked away from him. "Enjoy!"

"Thanks for checking out my skivvies."

Laughter filtered back as Elise disappeared down the hallway. Shaking his head, Samuel poked through the pile of clothing, already liking several pieces they'd picked out for him.

"Do you like the gift?"

Samuel lifted his gaze and found Dakota braced against the doorframe, hands shoved into his pockets. A white apron wrapped around his waist and a towel tucked in the waistband. There were a couple of stains across the usually pristine fabric. He wondered what the chef had got into within the kitchen.

"Well? Sorry we're a week behind with the welcome gift, but we weren't sure what to do with you," Dakota said with a grin.

"Whether to keep me or kick me out back to New York?"

"It was a hard decision. Someone suggested concrete shoes and a ride out into the gulf."

"Oh. You're going old-fashioned mob style with the removal of the interference."

"Considering you're a yank in the Deep South, I thought it would be appropriate."

"I take it the decision was overridden to keep me instead."

"Hmm. Other way would get us all in trouble if you were missing."

Samuel laughed as he rose to his feet and walked toward Dakota. He lifted on his toes and pressed their lips together, his gaze meeting Dakota's surprised one. Lowering back to the ground, he caressed Dakota's lower lip. "Thank you for the welcome gift. I do appreciate the clothes. You were correct—I did need some casual clothes."

Not moving from the door, Dakota held still as Samuel touched him. "I'm happy you approve of the clothes. I wouldn't want to ruin another pair of your pants on the beach."

Remembering the reason why his pants were sandy and soaked around the hem, Samuel chuckled and shrugged. He reached out and tugged on a corner of Dakota's apron.

"What's all over your apron?"

Dakota took the corner of the fabric from Samuel's grip to check it out. "Hmm, I must have splashed my mornay sauce for the seafood dish I'm creating for tonight."

"Mornay sauce? What is that? Is this a new seafood dish?"

"It's a white béchamel sauce, but a little thicker with cheese and milk. I'm going to pour it over a steamed mixture of blue crab meat, bay scallops and gulf shrimp. I'll finish it in a hot oven with a seasoned mix topping to brown before serving. Everything is set in a small one-serving baking dish. It's something I do once a month if I get a deal on the different ingredients."

"Sounds delicious, I hope I can try a bit."

"I'll set one aside for you."

"What are you serving with it?"

"For this dish, I'm thinking of a chilled orzo and wild rice salad and fresh steamed vegetables."

"Definitely sounds delicious."

"I hope it'll live up to my standards."

"I'm sure it will as does everything else I've had the pleasure of tasting."

Dakota dropped his gaze and gave him a small smile. "Thank you. Coming from you, I know it's a true compliment."

"It's the truth."

"Thanks. I'm glad you like the gift," he said and pushed away from the doorframe.

Samuel touched his shoulder. "Wait. I have a question before you leave."

Dakota turned back to look over his shoulder. "Go ahead."

Moving his fingers around Dakota's broad shoulder, Samuel caressed the side of his thumb against Dakota's neck. "What the hell do you do leaving at four a.m. every morning? I hear you moving about, the door closing, and you going down the hall. You said something about running on the beach and a swim. Is that all you do? Why would you run so early in the dark?"

"It isn't all I do. I actually go for a run and swim after my business."

"What kind of business gets done at four in the morning?"

"Restaurant business."

"Doing what?"

"Why do you want to know all of this?"

Samuel waved a hand back toward the covered desk. "I want to connect all these papers and numbers to what you do, what others in the hotel order, and additional things. I need your help to figure this out."

Dakota looked down at the floor and kicked his shoe against the frame. "I head down to the local fish market when the fresh catch is being brought in and priced. I also check out the local butchery and see their deals. I visit the farmers market and make deals for our fresh fruit and produce."

"Do you bring everything back?"

"No, the various markets will deliver it later in the day with the invoices. My staff will put them in their various compartments."

"What about bakery items?"

"We create our own fresh bakery items here. There's a back area devoted to our bakery of breads, rolls, pastries and desserts."

"When do you get sleep?"

"I can survive on four to five hours a night. When I get back, I set up a simple breakfast for the weekly staff meeting and a plain brunch table for the guests."

Samuel blinked at everything Dakota told him, more than he'd expected from him. "The staff meeting I walked in on while looking for coffee."

"Yes, we hold one every week at six to discuss the details of the week, leaving and arriving customers, and any other issues. It was something Edward and I used to keep in touch with everyone. I can put a cancellation notice on the board if you prefer until we finish sorting things, considering how the last one went."

"No. No. I would like them to continue. I wish to meet everyone and explain the situation."

"I'll make sure the meeting happens next week. This time you'll be on the notice."

"Appreciate it." Samuel nibbled on his lower lip.

"Anything else? I need to get back to the kitchen."

"One more thing."

"Okay. Which is?"

"Could I join you on your morning errands?"

Dakota braced a shoulder against the jamb and checked him over with a deliberate gaze. He traced his finger down Samuel's cheek. Samuel tried not to shiver under the rich, heavy gaze in those eyes and the gentle caress. "It depends."

"On what?"

"Can you get up?"

"If you'll bang on the wall between us to remind me and supply coffee, I will."

Dakota snorted. "We'll see."

"Is that a yes?"

"It depends on if you get up or not," he said as he turned and walked away from him. "I need to return to the kitchen. I'll send someone in with your dinner when it's ready."

"What the hell...?" Samuel shook his head as he walked back to the desk. "I'll never understand that man." He pushed aside the bags and plowed through the piles of paperwork, wondering if he would get anything accomplished.

Chapter Eleven

Managing to wake when ordered from pounding on their shared wall, Samuel yanked on clothes and stumbled down the stairs. He found a cheery, bright-eyed Dakota waiting for him in the kitchen.

Another yawn stretched his jaw with a popping motion before Samuel got hold of it and shook his head. Following Dakota outside, he drank another gulp of the strong, sugary black coffee Dakota had shoved in his hands. Still coming around, he didn't take much notice of the wild ride in the ancient Jeep. All he wanted was the blessed nirvana of caffeine to wake up his sluggish brain cells.

It's too damn early to be moving. Let alone to make important deals.

After the crazy ride, they stood on the docks in an active, bustling fish market lit by multiple flood lights against the darkness. They were still three hours ahead of dawn. He learned that the various local fishermen all turned their overnight catches in here for the best price.

Shoving his shoulder against the nearest post, he pressed fingers against his eyelids to counteract the achy, scratchy exhaustion which tugged at him. Samuel tried to concentrate on Dakota talking to the fish monger.

Is that the right word for the fish-smelling guy who walks around with a clipboard and acts like he owns everything? Samuel didn't know. At this point, he couldn't care less.

He scratched at the scruffy growth on his chin, he hated how out of sorts he felt in these yanked-on wrinkled jeans and shirt, and soft canvas sneakers. His hair was finger combed. His teeth felt fuzzy.

"Yuck…" Samuel pushed off one post and headed to another one closer to Dakota. He met the dead stare of some kind of fish.

Dakota walked back with the fish monger. "You're looking at dinner, Samuel. What do you think?"

"They're staring at me. It's creepy," Samuel said.

Dakota and the man laughed. They were far too awake and alert for him.

Samuel grumbled into the coffee cup. "What is it?"

"How can it be creepy? The fish is dead."

"Duh, I know that much. What kind of fish is it? Not awake and coherent here."

"That pile is mahi-mahi from the deep water of the bay. The one next to it is yellow-fin tuna. And the third pile is grouper," Dakota said.

"I read those on various menus I browsed, never saw them in the umm…scales." Samuel gave the large mouth grouper another grim look. "They look a little ugly."

"They're a nice mild firm fish which takes on whatever flavors you add to it."

"If you say so. The mahi-mahi is quite colorful, though."

"Hmm. They are a striking fish," Dakota said.

"They're acrobatic and swift in the water, a hard fish to catch, but we have some of the best anglers," the fish monger added.

"So, Frank," Dakota said, "we're good on the delivery of the mahi-mahi, tuna, grouper, small scallops, the royal red tail shrimps and the jumbo shrimp."

"We're good. Same price as always," Frank said in a slow, Southern accent. He wrote something on the clipboard and held it out for Dakota to look over and sign off on the bottom. He ripped out a yellow copy and gave it to Dakota.

"Thanks for the morning look, Frank," Dakota said as he shook hands with the man.

"Always glad to help out the Charm." Frank nodded in respect of sorts to Samuel. "Nice to meet you, sir."

"Same to you, Mr..."

"Frank, just call me Frank, sir." He headed off to process the order.

"Nice fellow," Samuel said.

"Been around longer around the market and knows everything when it comes to seafood." Dakota stopped in front of Samuel. Unlike Samuel, Dakota was dressed in board shorts, a button down shirt and comfortable leather sandals. His eyes were bright and alert.

"What?" Samuel asked with a little edge in his voice.

"Are you sticking around for the rest of my errands?"

"I haven't walked away yet. Where are we going next?"

"You sure you're up to this?"

"I'm still awake."

Leaning over, Dakota pressed a quick kiss to Samuel's lips. He winked at him. "Back to the Jeep and we're on to the next stop."

"Where?"

"Meat market," he called over his shoulder as he strolled away.

Samuel watched the tight, gorgeous rear. "If I say I'm looking at some grade A prime beef now, will you smack my head?"

Laughing, Dakota continued to walk away. "Get your lazy ass in gear or you're walking back to the Charm."

Scrubbing a hand over his face, Samuel groaned and quickened his shuffling pace. "Why are you so damn skippy in the morning?" He took another sip from the cup, but discovered he'd emptied the damn thing. He shook it to make sure, cursed, then tossed it into the nearest garbage can. "I need more coffee. What's on the receipt the fish man gave you?"

"I'm used to these hours," Dakota said he stopped by Samuel. He reached out and rubbed a hand over Samuel's midback. "Aww, is the poor city boy out of coffee?"

Samuel flipped him the bird.

Dakota chuckled. "I'm amazed how your brain jumps from needing coffee to a receipt this early. I'm impressed."

Samuel grumbled at him, but groaned at the light massage. "Don't keep me from my coffee. Time doesn't make a difference. It's been ingrained in me since birth to worry about business stuff."

"I wouldn't dare." Dakota pulled out the folded yellow carbon paper from his pocket and handed it to Samuel.

"What am I looking at?" Samuel checked out the cramped handwriting.

"It's what you're asking about. This is a purchase receipt of my request of the types I ordered which includes the quantity, and the wholesale price. He doesn't charge me a delivery fee since we're local. When we get the final bill, you can compare everything back to the receipt for verification." Dakota hopped into the old rusty Jeep Wrangler. Earlier, he'd removed the half metal doors and folded the soft top into the zippered pouch. Samuel studied the rust spots and obvious repairs, brushed his fingers against the edge of silver duct tape wrapped around the roll cage. "Duct tape? Don't you think we're past time to retire this thing to the junk heap?"

"Shush! Don't say such a thing about my girl? She has a few years left. We've been everywhere together and I'm not about to give her up because of a few dings. Get yer ass in here," Dakota said.

"I feel like I need a tetanus booster." Samuel climbed in the other seat. Now he was a little more awake, he looked for the seatbelt. "Where's the belt?"

"Broken." Dakota cranked the engine with a twist of a key. He patted the wheel when the engine coughed and turned over. "Ahh, there we go, my beauty of an old girl. Hang on, Samuel." He smoothly worked the pedals and shift of the gear stick as they shot backwards in the parking lot before changing gears to drive down the road.

"Broken? What do you mean broken?" Samuel clung to the 'oh-shit bar'. "Oh shit!"

"Why are you worried now? You already took a trip without it."

"I was half asleep. Why the hell can't we take my car?"

Dakota snorted. "Please. That's a damn toy."

"It's a work of art, unlike this thing."

"Again..." Dakota switched gears and pulled a hard turn to make Samuel tighten his grip on the bar. "Don't make fun of my baby."

"Just don't kill me," Samuel pleaded. "I need more coffee before I croak."

"Odd request, but doable," Dakota said with a wicked grin.

Grumbling, Samuel returned to try to concentrate on the flapping paper in his hand. He folded it a different way so he could see the scribble in Frank's cramped handwriting. He double checked the prices and lifted an eyebrow. "Are these considered high or low prices?"

"Seasonal prices within a ten dollar range. Seafood prices are always seasonal and availability priced and I don't question it."

"Why not? Haven't you bargained for better?"

"Not since Horizon. I trust Frank and vice versa. I did tell you how the man's been around forever, through all the shit that happened to the market." Dakota glanced at him. "I don't question the prices my friends give me. They cut close to their profit margins while working with mine."

"Okay. Okay. It's my position to check upon everything."

"Are you going to do this the entire time you're here?"

"Until I get things figured out and the numbers balanced, perhaps," Samuel said. "You owe me another coffee for dragging me out here."

"Umm, I believe you invited yourself." Dakota's Jeep screeched to a stop in a parking spot. "You can get coffee over there. I'll be in there." He pointed out the two storefronts.

"Is the coffee place open?" Samuel looked around. "Hey, this isn't a Starbucks? How can there not be a precious home of caffeine nirvana around?"

"Small seaside town which caters to tourists, but locals are here all year round. We don't care who creates coffee, but most of us don't have five bucks to waste on a latte."

Samuel whimpered.

"Chill. Head over to Breeze Shoppe. Candice and Neal run the place. They make awesome coffee from top beans they purchase from environmental growers. You can get just about everything and anything in there."

"I'll visit the fake coffee shop."

"Don't let them hear you call it that. I don't want to be kicked out of their place because you're ungrateful."

"Pot. Kettle."

"Yeah, yeah, behave yourself. They're good friends."

With another grumble, Samuel climbed out of the Jeep, patted his pocket to make sure he'd slid his wallet inside before leaving. He headed down the sidewalk.

"Meet me in the butcher shop."

Samuel waved a hand as he wandered down the sidewalk. He checked out the storefronts, some dark while others showed signs of getting ready for the new day. His phone rang shrilly from his pocket and he hooked his Bluetooth bud around his ear and hit the accept button.

"This is Samuel," he said.

"Morning, son. How has the week been?" his father said.

"The week has been busy, a little chaotic, a little tense, but I'm enjoying my time down here."

"It's to be expected. The employees are used to one way and you come in and change things up."

"A long battle and now I understand some of your grief and stress."

"Something you need to figure out on your own. What are you doing up this early?"

"Got dragged out of bed at four a.m. to accompany the co-owner and chef, Dakota Mitchell, to see what he does every morning. I'm checking out a few things in the small town called Shore Breeze. I watched him haggle and buy fresh caught seafood. Now he's about to do the same at a real butcher shop. I didn't think they existed any longer."

"You got up this early to follow him around. Sounds like a diligent young man."

"He insists on having only local seafood and produce in his dishes."

"It keeps the money circulating with the local area to keep everyone in business. It's a good practice. Make sure you keep this option available for any future changes."

"I will, sir."

"Do you have a moment to speak?"

"Yes, sir, I'm getting coffee at a local place called Breeze Shoppe before I return to watch him. This is a great small town near the ocean and has access to the bridge across the bay to Pensacola. I'm sure we will get great beach traffic once we get the right signage and promotions." Samuel stopped outside the store. "Did you get the emails about my initial thoughts and requests?"

"I'm reading through the latest one now, considering some options, and wanted to know more about some points."

"Sure... Go ahead." Samuel leaned against a post and listened to his father's concern. He pushed back his exhaustion to remember everything he'd learned to explain his points.

It took longer than expected to talk through the various points with his father. He glanced down the street and saw Dakota leaning against the front bumper of the Jeep. He lifted a finger for another moment and pointed to his ear. Dakota strolled down the sidewalk with the same, easy, hip-swinging walk. Before he could break and speak to Dakota, the man entered the store behind him.

"All right, son. I'll accept your view about those points. I'll speak with Chandler and send him down to you. You do know he'll not be happy he has to travel," his father said.

The tone in his father's voice altered when they changed the discussion to their eccentric accountant. Chandler was his best friend. His father never appreciated Chandler's work.

"I know, but I need him here to look at the books. I suspect most of the problems will lie within those pages and this bookkeeper fella. I want all the dots connected before making a formal accusation."

"You know how to handle him best along with his eccentricities. Go ahead with requests for construction, landscaping, and signs and get budgets and designs. I'll approve all orders and shift additional funds into the hotel's account, but you must have everything double signed by yourself and Mr Mitchell," his father said. "You were correct about needing time to decipher all the information."

"It was all due to Mom and her belief in this place."

"She has an excellent eye and business sense. Now, you need to accomplish everything you can to bring up the status and strength of this first hotel to our line. As for the local individuality and influence within the rooms and beyond the restaurant, I'm not sure. Let me think upon such ideas and work through some numbers. Considering the current problem of not knowing their accuracy, we may have to put it on the back burner until everything is addressed."

"Agreed, please do whatever you feel is best."

"Good work for your first week." His father, as usual, hung up before Samuel could thank him.

With a lengthy sigh, Samuel hit the button to turn off the ear bud. He saw a cup appear in front of his face and made a gimme motion with his hands. Turning to follow the cup, he saw Dakota standing next to him, sipping from another cup. He shifted both cups out of the way and planted a kiss on Dakota's surprised mouth.

Dakota responded with ease and took control of their kiss with a tilt of his head. A slide of his tongue against Samuel's lips and he deepened things between them. Since Samuel had his hands free, he tangled his fingers in Dakota's soft hair.

When they parted after a few heated moments, Dakota stared at Samuel. An amused smile was upon his lips. "I get a whopper of a kiss for a simple cup of coffee. Wow, I'm a lucky fella."

"Thank you, I need my caffeine." Samuel snatched one of the cups from Dakota with a wink. He took a long deep sip of the fresh brew.

"I should always bring you a cup of coffee if I keep getting a kiss."

"Perhaps, depends on the mood I'm in."

"Could it have been the phone call to set you off?"

"I apologize, I didn't expect him to call so early."

"It isn't a problem. Who was it?"

"My father."

"Ahh, he's your boss."

"With my mother, but yes, I answer to them. He wanted to discuss several emails I sent over last week," Samuel said. "Where do we go next for your errands?"

"Nope, no need, I finished my orders at the butcher shop and the farmers market. I got lucky since the butcher had an ample supply of ribs at a damn good price. We're gonna have a rib night. It's a popular event," Dakota said as he handed over two more yellow slips.

With a nod, Samuel looked over the slips, checked out the prices and amounts ordered. "Oh, I didn't realize I took so much time. I wanted to see both places."

"Next time."

"Sounds like a plan. When are you going to have this rib night? Tonight?"

"No, I want them for the main course on Friday. I like the ribs to marinate for at least twelve hours and go in for a long slow smoke. It'll take a good day and a half to get the smoker ready and hot enough to get a good smoke. The longer they sit in the smoke the more fall-off-the-bone tender they become."

"How does everyone know about this rib night?"

"We put up a couple of signs around and I'll call the local paper to run a promo. Leigh will get it in right away."

"You have a local paper."

"*Breezy Times*. It's a small paper with local news, fluff, promos for various businesses, and some outside information," Dakota said.

"Nice name for a little paper," Samuel said.

"We like it." Dakota led them back to the Jeep. "It's time to get back. I need to get in my run, swim and a nap before I begin the rest of my day."

"How do you do this? You're going for a run and a swim after all this? Nap... Oh, a nap sounds so good right now."

"I run along the beach for five miles and swim for a couple more. It's a great workout and helps keep me fit against all the food I enjoy."

Samuel glanced down the more than fit body as Dakota slid into the driver's seat. "You do more than run and swim." He reached out and squeezed Dakota's upper arm to test the biceps. "You have some muscle here."

"I lift heavy food and cast iron skillets all day around a lot of heat. I get a workout in the kitchen. Get in the Jeep."

Walking around the front, Samuel climbed in the passenger seat, careful of the hot cup. "Why do you do this every day? Get up this early, go out and haggle, take a run, and head back to the Charm."

"It's part of running a restaurant which relies on local products. I like knowing where my food comes from." Dakota drove down the single road out of the town. "I'm used to the hours."

"I need a couple more hours to feel human. Let alone the minimum needed to stare at those numbers." Samuel rubbed the bridge of his nose under his sunglasses. "The good news is my father agreed to send Chandler, and I can begin construction and landscaping repairs and create new signs."

"What kind of construction and landscape repairs? What the hell do you want to fix? You told me multiple things, but..."

"You told me you would try to remain open to the ideas and changes. Now I have approval, why do you want to throw roadblocks?"

"I'm not. I mean..." Dakota let out a sigh.

Chapter Twelve

Samuel waited for Dakota to decide on his words.

Dakota shifted gears as he drove down the local highway. "I didn't know you figured what changes to make. I heard nothing about this."

"You never asked."

"You didn't offer to talk and no, I didn't read all the memos you dropped on my desk."

"Okay. So we both screwed up."

"I thought it would take longer to make these decisions."

"We don't have the time to argue the finer points. Every day we lose business, it'll get harder to get out of the red. We need to push forward."

"Okay. Okay. I'm listening now so talk to me." Dakota glanced at him. "How much are we talking about?"

Samuel waited until Dakota had turned down the crazy road. "Slow down and stop. Let me show you how I see things."

Dakota grumbled, but stopped the Jeep and turned it off. "Go ahead."

"First, how is anyone going to find the Charm?"

"There are directions and GPS units."

"I used one and got lost."

Dakota blew out a heavy breath and ran a hand over his hair, messing the curls further. "What do you suggest?"

"Obvious—we need a sign. Several in fact since there's no signs from any street, especially this main one. Nothing to show anyone the Charm is down this road. We need to have signs both out here and up and down this main road, even in the town. We want to draw visitors to the Charm off the bridge and beach, and guide those who are looking for the place."

Crossing his arms over the wheel, Dakota looked around the area. "Agreed, I've told Edward for years we need more signs."

"Okay. I would like to have some created and installed. I'll start looking for a company who can design and build them. I need to check in Pensacola."

"What's next?"

Samuel climbed out of the Jeep and tugged Dakota with him. He stepped into the thick overgrowth and brushed his hand through it. "Look at this disaster around the road and the craziness of this untouched place. The road needs to be re-sloped, straightened and covered with new gravel, pavers, or something else. I would like all of this mess gone and repurposed into a gorgeous entrance." Samuel waved a hand around the untamed natural chaos. "We need to put forth a beautiful front. We'll go with Southern gentile and antebellum style which befits the beauty of the house. I love the graceful old oaks, those knobby trees with all the moss..."

"Cypress. Those are cypress trees with Spanish moss," Dakota said as he kicked a sandal through the grass.

"Cypress, fine, I like the magnolias, Italian cypress trees, and other southern plants. We need a landscape architect and horticulturist. I want them to go from the main road and all the way up to the hotel."

Dakota reached out and tugged on an overhanging branch. Samuel turned to watch the stretch and play of muscles across Dakota's chest and arm. His cock lengthened and pressed against the zipper.

"I don't know why Edward and Thomas stopped the landscaping out here. I remember talking to Thomas about why he didn't get things cleaned after the last storm. He said he'll get in touch with someone. I thought he would get Southern Haven on the job, but..."

"Obviously he did nothing about it. Now it's a disaster and we need to deal with it."

Dakota nodded and got back in the Jeep. "You better call Reece at Southern Haven. I'm sure he'll have a plan and want to get his hands on the mess."

"Let me finish explaining this and you can tell me about this Reece. Either way, my plan for later today is to start calling folks and getting bids. Drive farther down the road to the gate so you can see what I'm talking about," Samuel said as he climbed in the seat.

Dakota drove down to the next part, the Jeep tilting and jolting in the potholes. Samuel groaned with a raised eyebrow.

"Yeah, I know. Don't need to point it out. We need to fix the road. Reece will know who to call."

"Pull up here." Samuel pointed to the dilapidated stone fence and useless gate. "This sign is hopeless and in the wrong place. Why is it so far away from the road? There is this fence thing and the gate. Neither of one serves any purpose. There is no security. All of this would need to be figured out and replaced."

Dakota drummed his thumbs across the steering wheel.

"Beyond this fence, whatever we use to cover and fix the road will continue and become a designated and defined parking lot and driveway. If we keep the fountain, we need to think about a replacement. We can't keep it in this condition," Samuel said as Dakota drove past the old fence and around the circle to the parking lot.

"What's wrong with the building?"

"Look at the Charm with fresh eyes, my eyes and those of the visitors. Tell me what you see?"

With a groan, Dakota parked the Jeep. He leaned against the back bumper. Shoving hands in the pockets of his khaki board shorts, he stared at the graceful antebellum and plantation-styled, three-story building.

Samuel stood next to him, studying the man and not the building. "What do you see?"

"She's an old building, having been around for over a hundred years. She's still got beautiful, graceful lines. This old place has seen the test of time, weather, and especially hurricanes. She's got the bones of a gorgeous lady, but she needs some work." Dakota lifted his sunglasses and looked at Samuel. "It's the same on the inside. I know there are some issues."

"Now we need to fix these issues and bring her back to her glory days."

"Sully will take good care of her. As I mentioned, Reece at Southern Haven can handle the landscape."

"You mentioned Southern Haven earlier. Who are Reece and this company?"

"Reece Simpson created this local landscape company which goes beyond mowing grass and trimming bushes. He's a landscape architect, designer, and horticulturist and helps designs and maintains nature. He created Haven on the other side of town."

"Would he know ideas of what plants and trees would be best?"

"It's part of his specialty."

"You mentioned how you used Sully to create the addition to the restaurant. What's his company called?"

"He owns Tarleton Carpentry."

"After a nap, I'll give them a call. Are their numbers somewhere on my desk?" Samuel asked with a yawn.

"Yeah, they should be somewhere there. I'm gonna go for a run."

"I can't believe you're not tired. Anyway, we'll talk more when things become more concrete."

"Sounds like a plan." Dakota leaned toward Samuel, gave him a light kiss. "Go on and take a nap."

Samuel stepped toward the hotel, but looked over his shoulder. "Not coming upstairs to change?"

"No need since I wear board shorts underneath and my sneakers are in the back," he said, pointing a thumb toward the Jeep. "It's easier to keep everything I need for my morning exercise in a bag. I replace things as needed. I can dive into the ocean in most of my board shorts."

"Oh. Umm…" Samuel glanced at the hotel and back to Dakota.

"What is it?"

"No, nothing. I need to drop these off. Never mind, I'll bring them to my room and put them with others. You have more of these invoices?" Samuel waved the three yellow slips.

"For every order, I do."

"Organized?"

Dakota glanced at him with a raised eyebrow.

"It's more along the lines of wishful thinking. I'll look through the piles." Samuel rocked back and forth on his toes.

"Are you sure that's it?"

"Yes, thank you again." Samuel waved to him. "Night...Erm, morning. I'll see you later. Have a good time on your run."

"Thanks. I will." Dakota remained against his Jeep, one hand in a pocket.

Wishing he was a little tougher to offer the man a different way to exercise, Samuel grumbled and headed inside. Moving upstairs, he fumbled for his key then unlocked his door. Samuel yawned and entered the cool room. He closed the door with a kick, toed off his shoes, and stripped his clothes.

"Stupid idiot," he muttered in no rational fashion as he dropped forward on the bed. "You could have had Mr Hot Chef in your bed, keeping you awake, and going beyond a beachside blow job. Instead you couldn't open your mouth and invite him for a better kind of exercise. Nope. Kept your mouth shut. Now, you have to sleep alone while Mr Sexy Body is running on the beach." He punched the pillow into submission, fluffed it, and face planted deep in the pillow. He let out a long groan of frustration. His cock was thick, aching, and pressed uncomfortably and rigid between his belly and the bed.

There was a knock on his door and Samuel turned his head. "Who is it?"

"Dakota."

"I thought you were going for a run."

"Would you come to the door? Please?"

Samuel's eyebrows lifted high toward his hairline at the word 'please' from the man. He wiggled out from under the covers, yanked on his boxers, and went to the door. After unlocking, he opened it a crack to stare at the taller man. "Did you forget something?"

"Yeah, I wasn't happy with the earlier one, so here's this..." Dakota put his hand out and threaded his fingers through Samuel's hair. He tugged Samuel onto his toes as he bent forward. He captured Samuel's open mouth, slid his tongue against the plump softness, and kissed him hard and deep.

When Dakota pulled back, Samuel grasped hold of his soft cotton shirt. "Don't go running. Come inside with me."

"Are you sure? Do you have stuff?"

Samuel nodded and shook his head. "Shit, I only have lube. I don't have condoms. I wasn't expecting to find someone to have sex with down here."

"Go inside, I have some next door." Dakota stepped back, waited for Samuel to release him, then moved away.

With some deep breathing, Samuel returned to the bed. He couldn't believe they were doing this. Hell, both of them had masturbated enough since the first day they'd met. The attraction sizzled between them even if they snapped at one another. Shoving fingers through his hair, he made his decision to accept whatever Dakota offered him. He dug under his pillow to find the lube he stashed there, and set it on the nightstand. He dropped back on the bed. He kept his gaze on the door as he drew his fingers down his chest. His heart raced with the growing arousal and excitement of a new lover. He wanted to wrap his fingers around his cock, but held off.

The door opened and Dakota stepped inside, a box in his hands. When he glanced at Samuel on the bed, there was a grin on his lips. Dakota reached back to lock the door. Stepping out of his loafers, Dakota walked over and set the box next to the pump bottle.

Snagging the back of his T-shirt, Dakota tugged it over his head and tossed it aside. He leaned over and nuzzled Dakota's mouth. Sharing a deep and varied explorative kiss, Dakota pulled back to lick Samuel's bottom lip, asking permission to dip inside.

With a moan, Samuel lifted his head, but Dakota gently pushed him back.

"No, just feel, let me lead," he whispered to him, his Southern drawl deeper and richer.

"I want..."

"I know," Dakota said as he settled on the edge of the bed. He brought his lips back to Samuel's mouth.

Samuel opened to the gentle, slow invasion, felt Dakota flick his tip against the roof of his mouth. It was a different, erotic form of the classic soul kiss. He moaned and sucked on Dakota's tongue, urged him to go further. Dakota gave him a few deeper licks before he pulled back and nibbled on his lower lip.

Dakota moved down to lavish attention on the rest of Samuel's face and body. He nibbled on his lip again, before he licked the tip of his nose with a laugh, then smeared a kiss down the length of Samuel's neck to the hollow above his clavicle. He lifted his mouth and kissed him deep again, before moving to nibble on his lobe.

Samuel shuddered when Dakota pulled back and exhaled a soft warm breath of air onto his moist skin. His body melted under the tender assault.

Again, Dakota moved and licked down Samuel's cheekbone, nipped his chin, and smeared another kiss over his throat. He licked around Samuel's prominent Adam's apple and he hummed in pleasure.

"You like…" Dakota whispered.

"Yes. Don't… Don't stop," Samuel said as he gripped the sheet.

"Reach back and take hold of the bars. Don't let go," Dakota said.

Samuel glanced behind him, saw the bars connecting to the headboard, and reached back. He gripped a bar in each fist. His body stretched out in front of Dakota.

"Damn, you look gorgeous like that. Love watching your muscles move. Can I top you?" Dakota drew a finger down the center of Samuel's chest.

"Yes," Samuel said on a whisper of air. "Can I enter you later?"

"Later." Dakota pulled his finger back up Samuel's chest, between the pecs, and circled the hollow between the collarbones. "Don't let go or I stop what I'm doing."

Samuel licked his lips.

"Good, enjoy," Dakota said as he leaned down again, before nibbling and licking Samuel's neck. He nuzzled a hairy armpit to breathe in Samuel's scent. "Hmm. Damn good smell on you." He licked around the edge.

Samuel wiggled and chuckled. "You're crazy."

"It's a known aphrodisiac to gay men."

"Yeah…I thought I read something about…" Samuel moaned when Dakota licked his skin again. "Damn…"

"Shush." Dakota gave him another contemplative kiss, delving deep. He moved across the erogenous zones of his nipples, licking around the darker skin, before flicking the bumps.

Samuel moaned under the attention, his cock rigid within the confines of his boxers.

Dakota moved below the ridge of muscles. He followed the single line of body hair tapered down the middle of Samuel's chest. He licked across his tummy Samuel worked hard to keep flat. He flicked his tongue a few times around Samuel's navel. Samuel shivered as Dakota explored his body. Dakota nuzzled around the waistband of the boxers before he spent time on both of Samuel's legs. He tilted one to nip the back of the nearest knee.

"Let's remove these, shall we?" Dakota tucked his fingers into the waistband, pulled the cotton boxers down, and tossed them aside.

Samuel's erection bobbed, released by the cloth, until it curled toward his belly. He moaned as he arched his back. Dakota skimmed his fingers across Samuel's legs, brushing over the dusting of curls.

"Hmm, thank you for keeping some body hair. It's not natural for us to be so smooth. I noticed you wax your balls, but leave this little tuft of hair above your cock. Nice," Dakota said as he let his fingers drift across Samuel's hips and pelvis. He stretched out on his side, leaned in and kissed him.

As their kiss deepened and Samuel became more aroused, Dakota trailed his fingertips along the sensitive flesh of his belly. Samuel moaned under the kiss. His hips shifted on the bed, fluid leaked from his cock tip. Dakota pulled back, traced the outline of Samuel's kiss-swollen mouth, even brushed in to touch his teeth. He brought his fingers to his mouth and licked them while keeping his gaze on Samuel.

"Oh, damn..." Samuel whispered when those wet fingers drew lines down his stomach, through the fluff of hair and around his rigid cock. He moaned when

Dakota grazed his cock with the side of his hand before grasping the base.

Sweat covered his body as he moaned under Dakota's sensual touch. He groaned when Dakota blew a cool stream of air over his body and followed with light, sensitizing flicks.

"Oh, damn... Please..."

Dakota shifted and bent over him. He grasped the base of Samuel's cock and licked around the ridge. He dipped and moved his tongue around the responsive skin between the head and shaft. Dakota hummed against the skin. Samuel cried out in pleasure and tightened his grip until his knuckles whitened. He wanted to sink them into Dakota's hair.

Dakota wrapped his lips around Samuel's cock and sucked him in earnest. He worked one hand over Samuel's shaft and held his free hand above Samuel's belly.

"Squeeze lube on my fingers," he ordered.

Licking his lips, Samuel forced his fingers to release the bars, fumbled for the bottle, and pumped some cool liquid on Dakota's fingertips.

"Good, now return your hands to grasp the bars."

Samuel dropped the bottle against his hip and reached behind him.

With a smile, Dakota worked the lube between his fingers and lowered his mouth around Samuel's cock. He slid his greased fingers under Samuel's smooth balls, and gently stroked the perineum from the scrotum to Samuel's ass cheeks. Samuel whimpered when Dakota touched his heated skin.

Continuing to suck Samuel's cock, Dakota pressed a finger around the rim of Samuel's ass—circled his sphincter a couple of times until he relaxed. After another outstroke, Dakota stuck a lubed finger inside

Samuel's ass. He cried out with pleasure as a second finger joined the first. Dakota's hand moved from his shaft to fondle his balls. Closing his eyes, Samuel climaxed hard and strong. He called out Dakota's name. He shot streams of cum into Dakota's mouth. His hips bucked off the bed to force his cock deeper, but the man held him down.

When his balls emptied, Samuel felt his cock soften and slip out. He managed to crack open his eyes to see Dakota lick his lips.

Dakota slipped his fingers inside Samuel's ass, opening him, preparing him. "Ready for more..."

Samuel nodded.

Dakota slid his fingers free and yanked off his shorts. Reaching for the box, he yanked out a foil packet and sheathed himself. He pumped more lube on his fingers to slick his cock.

"Spoon me," Samuel said as he released his grip on the bars. "Please..."

"I can't see you..."

"Too much for me... Please..."

"This time," Dakota said and helped Samuel roll to the side. Spooning against him, they situated their legs to twine together.

As they curled around each other, Samuel glanced over his shoulder to stare at Dakota. Dakota slid his fingers back inside Samuel's ass. He moaned as Dakota nudged his gland. Dakota lined up his prepared cock.

"Push back against me as I enter," Dakota said.

While Dakota entered him, Samuel concentrated on relaxing and pushing back to accept the thick length. He groaned at the exquisite stretch of his ass. Dakota thrust forward to slide in farther. He angled his hips and shifted back to help the man go deeper. Dakota bottomed out. He tilted his head until their lips met in a desperate kiss.

"Fuck me… Hard," Samuel pleaded.

"Whatever you wish," Dakota said, placing a hand on Samuel's hips, before he began to thrust smooth, deep and hard. Keeping his rhythm, he fondled Samuel's cock.

Once again, Samuel climaxed and called out in pleasure. His ass squeezed and clamped around Dakota's cock. Dakota thrust with a cry as he released and filled the condom. Sweaty, exhausted, Samuel groaned, his body sore from the exercise. Dakota pulled out and dealt with the condom.

Samuel heard the condom drop in a container and grimaced at the mess. "Ick…"

"Hmm. Come back from the wet spot. We'll clean up later," Dakota said, kissing Samuel's shoulder as they shifted on the bed. He wrapped his arm and leg around Samuel, spooning and cuddling him against his larger frame. Their hands intertwined as they shared the same pillow and drifted into slumber.

Chapter Thirteen

After a nap, Dakota woke Samuel with kisses and nibbling on his earlobe. He snagged a couple of condom packets and dragged Samuel into the shower. He turned the knobs, hearing the protest of the old pipes, and found some towels. After tossing the packets on the counter, he whipped open the curtain and pushed Samuel underneath the spray.

"Ahh! Cold!" Samuel jumped back from the icy spray and fixed the knob. "Are you mad? Damn, my nuts were about to freeze off."

"Woke you up," Dakota teased as he nipped at his ear.

"The wrong way, pal, entice me with a kiss, coffee or bacon. I prefer it in that precise order too."

"I'll remember your personal recommendations for future engagements," Dakota said as he pushed Samuel forward until the spray hit him full force. This time it was warmer as the water heater cranked and got to work.

Pressing his hands against the tile, Samuel ceded to the gentle ministrations. Dakota soaped and scrubbed down Samuel's scalp with the fragrant citrus shampoo, massaged his fingers through his hair. After the heat and intensity of sex, Dakota enjoyed this softer, quieter side of a relationship, not that he had one with Samuel. Hell, he wanted to release the tension and attraction between them in a healthy way. Still, the way Samuel opened up to him was fabulous to watch. He adored how the golden caramel eyes darkened as Samuel's passion and attraction rose.

"Gonna leave me soapy?" Samuel asked, his sleepy voice tugged Dakota from his thoughts.

"Nah, sorry," Dakota said and gently pushed Samuel under the water and helped to rinse his hair clean. He found the loofah and soaked it with water and gel. He started a thorough head to toe wash over his new lover, front and back. While he worked, Samuel's cock became harder, and pressed his ass against Dakota's thigh.

"Please... Again..." Samuel pleaded.

"So demanding," Dakota teased as he hung the loofah, squeezed a little gel on his fingers, and pushed fingers into Samuel.

"More... Get inside me." Samuel pushed his ass back against Dakota's fingers.

"Shit... Condom..." Dakota stretched a hand around the curtain to grasp a foil packet. After using his teeth to open the darn thing, he rolled it over his cock, added more gel to the latex, and pushed inside Samuel. He groaned when Samuel gripped his head. "Damn, you're so tight. This is going to be fast."

Samuel moved a leg, and helped Dakota sink farther into him. "Move. Please..."

Dakota slapped Samuel's ass cheek.

Samuel yelped.

"I'm in control. You enjoy," Dakota said.

"Gonna get you back."

"Look forward to it. Now, it's my turn." He gripped Samuel's hips and increased the pace and tension of his thrusts. He shifted his angle to make sure he hit the prostate and make Samuel's eyes cross with pleasure. "Damn, you feel so good." Dakota lowered his head to press his face against Samuel's neck. He couldn't believe how perfect Samuel was as they came together.

Samuel shouted out as his cum splashed against the tiles. His ass clamped around Dakota's cock. Dakota shot his load deep in the condom. They collapsed against each other. Dakota wrapped an arm around Samuel's waist to hold them upright. He placed a hand on the wall.

"Oh damn, what a way to wake up," Samuel said with a groan.

"Hmm. I enjoyed it. It's something I could get used to doing every morning," Dakota said as he kissed the nape of Samuel's neck.

"Later, I want a chance to take control," Samuel said, lifting his hand to sink his fingers into Dakota's hair. He tilted his head to the side, giving Dakota more room to kiss him.

"Yeah, I want to feel you slide inside me." Dakota held the condom as he pulled out then tossed it in the garbage. Samuel switched places.

"Your turn to get clean," Samuel said and pushed Dakota under the spray.

Laughing together, they finished cleaning one another in the shower in between spats of kissing, groping and spurting water out of their noses and mouths. Leaving Samuel alone to change, Dakota wrapped a towel around his waist, gathered his clothes, and returned to his room.

* * * *

Dakota found himself all smiles as he worked. He'd called a couple of folks in early to help with the rib night prep and he had his barbecue guru, Peter, downstairs with the old smoker. He'd left the man alone while he filled it with large amounts of hickory, oak and other woods to build a steady, warm fire for a long cook. Peter and another man would take turns throughout the night watching the ribs and fire.

In the main kitchen, Dakota had numerous spices and portions of his special rub spread out in front of him. He chose a large bowl to dump everything in and mix. Two assistants worked on cleaning and prepping the newly arrived ribs, spacing them out on tinfoil covered pans.

Dakota measured, tossed and mixed a dry rub. He followed it by creating a basting sauce. He would spritz and turn the ribs a couple of times while they sat in the fridge, absorbing all the goodness before they smoked. Peter would baste them as they cooked. He yanked off and threw away the dirty gloves. He placed the various containers back to their positions or in the cleaning station.

"Are the ribs ready for the rub? Do we have room in the cooler?" Dakota asked his assistants. He noticed his seafood chef, Glenn, helped with the all hands on deck process.

Glenn pulled a large metal rolling cart with several shelves from a storage area. "This can fit. I made room before getting this baby out."

"Good. Good."

"Here, start with these pans. They're all trimmed and ready for your special care," Mal said as he slid the trays down the table.

"The longer these babies marinate with the rub, the better they get. Glenn, grab a new pair of gloves and help Mal prep. I'll deal with the rub," Dakota said as he tugged out a fresh pair of gloves. He grabbed a handful of the rub and massaged it into the meat.

A few hours later, all three men rubbed and massaged the ribs and covered them with the basting sauce. They wrapped layers of tinfoil around the trays and placed them on the cart.

Dakota lobbed the gloves toward the trash. Glenn pushed the heavy cart into the cooler. Dorian dealt with the mess left behind, cleaning everything to a sparkle.

"When you're done, Dorian, find the signs and put them all out in the usual spots. Make sure everything says Friday night, not before," Dakota said as he moved to the corner desk and pulled down his recipe book.

"You got it, Chef," Dorian answered.

Glenn backed out of the cooler, closed the door, and yanked off his gloves. "Man, those are gonna be good. Hope there's some for us."

"Yeah, same here," Dorian said as he left the kitchen.

"What are we going to put out with them?" Mal leaned against the counter next to Dakota.

"Thinking our sweet potato fries and hickory baked beans."

"Do we need to do this now or wait?"

"Let's do the prep work now."

"Okay, I'll slice the fries and get the beans in a bowl of water," Mal said.

"Put Dorian on the fries. You can handle getting the beans together. Do we have enough hickory smoked bacon?"

"Let me check the cooler." Mal pushed off to check the correct walk-in cooler. "Yeah, we got a few pounds of the thick-cut style."

"Great, I want it cubed and added in the pots. The beans will sit on the smoker with the ribs overnight."

Mal hefted out the package of bacon and set it on a table. He used a cart to haul out the large baskets of sweet potatoes and left them by the slicer for Dorian. He went into the dry pantry and grabbed the large bags of beans along with several bowls.

Dakota located his pad and pen and created menus for the next two days along with the Friday rib night. This was both the fun and irritating part as he figured out how to break down the ingredients into various meals which would be profitable.

"What's for tonight?"

"I'll create a seafood brodetto with the shrimp, scallops, and grouper. I've been toying with it, different from gumbo, and a different fare than usual. We have our usual tea-soaked chicken but I'll put it with the fresh zucchini and squash ribbons."

"Ribbons?"

"You slice them lengthwise with a peeler to create ribbons like pasta."

"Oh. Right. Sorry."

"No problem. Glenn, can you handle the seafood?" Dakota asked the older man.

"Can do," Glenn said with a nod.

"Mal, I want you and Dorian on the ribbons. I'll show you the technique I want used on them," Dakota said.

Mal nodded in agreement.

Dakota scribbled and made notes of who was handling what in prep and time. "We'll do a shrimp scampi with the royal red tails with fresh linguini. I'll hold the jumbo shrimp for Monday's gumbo and pick up the rest of the ingredients."

Mal tapped his fingers on the counter as he listened. "What about a vegan dish?"

Dakota flipped through his recipe book and tapped the pen as he looked through the various sheets he'd gathered throughout his years as a chef. "I could make a vegetable curry with jasmine rice."

"Curry sounds good. I love a good curry," Samuel answered.

Dakota looked over his shoulder. Samuel entered the kitchen, looking fresh and relaxed after their late morning nap and joint shower. He couldn't hide the smile that appeared at the sight of him. "Hey there. Did you decide to venture out of your cave?"

"Yes, I needed a break. By the way, the curry does sound like a good idea. I haven't had one in a while." Samuel looked around the kitchen.

"Okay, we'll go with a curry. It'll be an interesting mixture of palates tonight." He wrote down the titles and pulled out the coordinating recipes from his book. "Need to set up the brodetto and curry first. They'll do better with longer cooking times. Glenn, can you switch to getting the curry together first and go to the ribbons. Pull out the baskets of sweet onions, garlic, cauliflower, sweet potatoes, tomatoes, carrots, and cans of chickpeas. Also grab the gingerroot. Start prepping all those vegetables."

Glenn waved a hand to show he'd heard the change of prep and grabbed a cart before he disappeared into the various coolers and pantry for the list of ingredients.

Leaning against one of the tables, Samuel listened while Dakota spoke a few things to Mal and added them to his notes. "Have a question for you."

"Sure. Fire away."

"Once you figure out the menu, you work on the price points of everything to come up with a final total of cost. How much do you charge the customer?"

"I try to figure it out. Most costs are in my head, but I work on them."

"It's an interesting way to figure out things. With a regular set menu, you know what to charge them every night and how much the dish costs."

"We have a couple of things which we put on the menu all the time. The chicken dish is popular, our appetizers are the same, and the drinks don't change."

"So you do try to keep some bases to work with when you're creating new menus. It's good to know," Samuel said. He traced a finger around one of the patterns in the created stone counter. "Would you like some good news?"

"I can't stop anytime soon for a little break," Dakota said with a grin.

"Darn," Samuel said and snapped his fingers. "I meant good news concerning business."

"Sure. Go ahead. Perhaps I can sneak back to the office later."

"Should I make sure to stash supplies?"

"It's a good idea to have supplies everywhere. We'll have to work on your delightful noises. Things aren't well insulated down here."

"Hey, I'm not loud."

Dakota lifted an eyebrow.

"Okay. Okay. I'll grab a couple of throw pillows or something."

"I'll find a way to keep your mouth occupied. Figuring out how to stick a comfortable chair in there would be helpful, too."

"There isn't much in the way of wall space or a free area."

"I'll have to see the layout of my room." Dakota shrugged and pushed it aside. "What's this news?"

"I got in touch with your friend Sully, and he's agreed to come over tomorrow or the next day, discuss a few options, and look over the Charm to create a budget. He gave me the name of a company who can handle the entire driveway, a fence supplier and a security company. I called all three and they'll also be coming over within the next few days, before the weekend for sure."

"Looks like it'll get busy around here. We need to accommodate what guests we have."

"I know and I'll make sure they're not too bothered by the activity. Anything requiring more noise or annoyance scheduled for days when there aren't guests. I contacted Ashford's preferred option to handle websites, advertising and social media interests. They're going to send someone to look over the Charm, rebuild the website and set up a comprehensive advertising plan."

"Sounds like you've been busy these last couple of hours."

"My nap was energizing so I got a lot accomplished. My Bluetooth yapped in my ear from the moment I came downstairs." Samuel rubbed the offended ear in question. "I left a message for Southern Haven and for Reece to contact me when available."

"Reece's probably on a site somewhere."

"I didn't have a cell phone so we'll have to wait. Is Reece a local?"

"Nah, Reece came here from somewhere in Northern California, I think."

"Reece is too cute under all the dirt and grime. Sigh, I do wish he would see me," Mal said patting a hand over his heart.

"Dork...I told you to talk to him." Dakota wadded a paper towel, tossed it, and beaned Mal on the head with near perfect aim.

"Me? How can I talk to Reece? Are you bonkers?" Mal lobbed the towel back. "He's drop-dead, pure perfection, of six-foot-plus gorgeous male. I'm..." Mal waved a hand down his slender, petite frame. "I'm a nerdy sous chef who prefers a night watching *Firefly* reruns when I'm not getting sweaty dancing in a crowded club. These are two different sides to what makes up the variety and pizzazz you see here."

"Damn good show, I miss Captain Mal," Samuel said with a grin.

"I know. My namesake is gorgeous," Mal said with a flip of his hair.

Samuel laughed.

Dakota turned when the door to the kitchen opened.

"Hey, Chef, all signs are out. The one in town is already getting views," Dorian said with a chuckle as he headed to the sink for a wash. "Oh, hello there. You must be the new owner, I'm the prep cook, but training to be a line chef. I'm Dorian Stewart." Dorian dried a hand and held it out to Samuel.

"Samuel Ashford. Thanks and good to meet you, Dorian," Samuel said with a quick shake.

"Sorry, gotta wash again. Food prep rules. Where do you want me, Chef?" Dorian dried off with fresh towels. He slipped his apron on over his clothes.

"I need you to send those sweet potatoes through the fry cutter. We need shoestring fries in the oven tomorrow. Toss them with paprika, cumin, and salt before you stick them in the cooler."

"You got it."

"Report to Glenn after he finishes the curry and together you'll create vegetable ribbons out of the squash and zucchini."

"You do them with a peeler, right?"

"Yeah. Whoever comes in next will get on them if Glenn is tied up with the curry and you can finish helping them when you're done."

"Got it, Chef. Busy afternoon," Dorian said. "Want the skin on with those fries?"

"Yes, but give them a good scrub with the brush."

Dorian raised a hand as he headed to his station to prep the potatoes and workspace.

Samuel watched the young cook. "Seems like a good fellow."

"Dorian's been with us since he was a teenager. He took a job as a dishwasher. Over the years, I helped him learn the rest. Now he's one of my best preppers."

"Is he planning on attending culinary school?"

"It's in his plans, but his mother is ill with MS and he doesn't want to leave her in a hospice. He couldn't afford one if he tried to find a place for her. His father died of cancer and he's an only kid. Glenn, Mal, and I do what we can to help them out since they're swamped with medical bills," Dakota said. "He's a damn good kid. He's only nineteen."

"I thought he was older," Samuel said. "I'll see what we can do for him and his mom."

"Edward set up what he could, but better access to health insurance would be helpful."

"Once the hotel has been acquired, we'll allow employees to join our health care plans within six months. I'll see what we can do to waive the time for

Dorian and his mom and figure out a way around her pre-existing condition."

Dakota stopped what he was doing and looked at Samuel. "Thank you. It would go a long way to helping them." Seeing Mal kid around with Dorian, Dakota rolled his eyes. "Mal!"

Mal jumped like a scared rabbit. "What? I didn't do anything."

"Exactly." He waved Mal back to his work. "Get those vegetables diced fine for the brodetto."

"Yes, maestro slave driver," Mal said with a low, teasing bow. "Do you want the trio of carrots, onions, and garlic?"

"Yes. Make sure it's a fine dice!"

"I know. I know." Mal headed to the produce cooler with a rolling cart. He bumped shoulders with a chuckling Dorian. He waved as the back door opened and a couple entered. The young lady was the pastry chef while her boyfriend was another prep cook. "Hey, you guys. Chef, Kristen and Eric are here."

"Good. Kristen, get on dessert of berry tarts and chocolate silk mousse. Eric, wash up and get with Dorian. He'll show you what we need tonight," Dakota called to the newcomers.

"Yes, Chef!" both said at the same time and split in different directions after a quick kiss of affection.

"You're getting busy in here," Samuel said.

"We'll be like this until dinnertime hits. It's why I prefer to have dinner service for those outside the hotel, but we offer meals throughout the day to guests."

"Speaking of a meal, could I get something I can snack on in my office?" Samuel rubbed a hand against his belly. "I worked up an appetite."

"I got some chicken salad in the cooler. I can whip you up a quick sandwich."

"Perfect. No nuts?"

"None. I put sliced grapes, diced pears, carrots, and onion in it. It has a Greek yogurt base."

"Sounds divine. I'll take a whole one. Any chance you have chips?"

"A couple of bags are in the pantry. Go snag the flavor you want. I'll make us both a sandwich since I haven't had anything either."

"Sweet. Thanks! I want some of the tea too!"

"You do like our tea," Dakota said with a chuckle. "Tea is in the first fridge and pitchers are above the drink station. Go and help yourself."

"I'm addicted to it. I believe it's about as good as your coffee." Samuel went to the pantry and whistled.

"What?"

"Damn, you have a helluva lot of food. This is a good size area."

"Yeah, we'll use all of it and more."

"Hey, you're organized here, why not in your office?"

The rest of the kitchen crew laughed.

Dakota grumbled while he constructed several sandwiches. Samuel tossed several bags of chips on the counter and helped to pour glasses of tea. Dakota finished each plate with a pile of potato chips. After ordering his crew to get their laughing asses to eat and get back to work, Dakota followed Samuel to Samuel's office. He dropped in the visitor chair and balanced the plate on his lap.

"Did I say the wrong thing?" Samuel asked after eating a few bites of his sandwich.

"No, it's an ongoing joke between the kitchen crew and Edward. He often discussed the same thing, but he wasn't any better. In a kitchen, you need to keep everything organized to make sure all the ingredients stay fresh, clean, and don't cause contamination. I know kitchens and where to put things. In an office..." Dakota waved at the covered desk. "I have no clue. I know the basics, but not everything. I didn't go to culinary school for restaurant management."

"Don't worry, I can figure out the paperwork. I'm good at organizing. Chandler will be a big help when he arrives."

"Is he coming?"

"Yes, I spoke with him after my dad gave him the news. He's interested in the books, but hates traveling."

"Why does he hate it?"

"He's...eccentric," Samuel said. "I believe he suffers from OCD and anxiety issues. Traveling and strange places makes it worse. He'll bring personal items to place about the room and office. Please try not to move anything once he places things as he requires. I'll make sure the maids don't touch his room."

"It sounds like he has a rough time."

"He does and I didn't want to bother him, but I need his expertise. He's a genius with numbers, no one better."

"We'll do our best to accommodate him. Should I have one of the ladies remove all the flowers and toiletries?"

"Please. If possible, we'll give it a thorough deep clean before his arrival. If you have a plain white comforter, sheets, blankets, and pillow cases, place them on the bed. He'll make it himself. Too much color disturbs him."

Dakota lifted an eyebrow, a chip held in front of his mouth.

"I know. Over the years of working with him, I learned some of his nuances. Though there are many more issues he keeps to himself. He's embarrassed or ashamed. He hasn't been able to keep a boyfriend since none of them can keep his issues straight or handle him."

"So… He's gay?"

"Yes. He grew up in a cluttered home. His mother was an extreme hoarder. I mean rooms filled to the ceiling like in those television shows. She was one of them, but never accepted or wanted help. Instead of falling into her pattern, he went into the extreme opposite by maintaining rigid control. Even when he moved out of the house, his brain was wired to keep things perfect."

"Damn. I don't know what I would do if I came from such a home. No wonder he's a little different." Dakota shook his head. "Thanks for letting me know about him."

"I don't like him to walk into strange situations."

"You're a good friend to him."

"I accept all of him. I hope some guy can see his uniqueness and adore him."

After cleaning off his plate, Dakota drank the rest of his tea and rose to his feet. "I need to get back to prep. Let me know if you need anything else. Are you done with your plate?"

"Yes, I'll keep the glass," Samuel said as he ate the last few chips and handed the plate over. "It's a wonderful sandwich. Thank you."

"Anytime you need something, just ask." Dakota stepped around the desk. "Have fun with your paperwork."

Samuel chuckled and shook his head. "I could pass some over to you."

"No. Thanks. No." Leaning over, Dakota captured Samuel's mouth in a heated kiss.

Samuel lifted his fingers to hold the back of Dakota's head as he continued their kiss. He nipped and pulled on the man's lower lip then released it with a grin. "Hmm. Sure you can't stay?"

"Not this time. It's a memento to think about for later." Reaching out, he picked up the pitcher and shook it. "I'll refill your pitcher to keep you going."

"Ooh, more caffeine and sugar. Just what I need."

Dakota snorted.

"I'll update you after dinner," Samuel called out.

"Sounds good."

Samuel admired the tight ass as Dakota disappeared down the hall. He enjoyed remembering how he'd sunk his fingers into those glorious muscles during their steamy shower and sighed. He turned his attention back to the numerous piles of paperwork scattered across the desk. He shifted again when his rigid cock pressed against the zipper. When it wouldn't go down, he shoved a hand down his pants, cursed the potency of Dakota's kiss, and rearranged himself.

Chapter Fourteen

Two more days had whipped past Samuel in a blur while he had delved deeper into the various paperwork piles, adding them to the cabinets, and trying to make some sense from everything he was reading. There had been the nights. Oh man, those delicious nights where he'd heated the sheets with Dakota. *Damn, he does know how to make love to a man.* A quiet smile curled his lips as he thought about the various positions they'd twisted each other into last night. His back was a little kinked and protested, but hell, he'd never come harder.

"Hey there, Dakota said to drop this off for you. A fan of our tea, huh?" Dorian said as he entered the office and set down a small tray with a pitcher of tea and a small bucket of ice.

"Yes, it's wonderful stuff. Thank you, Dorian."

"Got quite the mess here, huh?"

"I'm working my way through the piles, but I'll get there eventually."

"Hope you will. I don't want to see the Charm close down. I love this place. I hope I can stay here as long as possible."

"I'm hoping to find the solution so nothing happens to the Charm or any of your jobs." Samuel lifted his head and breathed in deep. "Damn, I smelled those ribs all day and my mouth is watering. What is his secret?"

"Chef says it all starts with the dry rub and the liquid basting throughout the smoke. No matter what he does, they go fast. Once the doors open, we'll be packed and nonstop. We go until we sell out," Dorian said with a wide grin.

"Do you sell out every time you barbecue ribs?"

"Yup, it's a total madhouse. It's all we offer on the menu with the sides. No one wants anything else when we have a rib special."

"Sounds like a good way to push sales."

"Hmm, but it's a lot of work to get all the orders out. Guess I better get back before Chef hollers my name." Dorian left the room.

Samuel chuckled as he poured more tea into his cup. Before he could take a sip, the phone rang through the intercom.

"This is Samuel," he said.

"Hello, Sullivan Tarleton is here. Should I lead him on back?" Elise said in her bright, cheerful tone.

"Ahh, I was expecting him. Yes, please, thanks, Elise."

Samuel rose and went to the guest chairs. He gathered the mess of paperwork from the seats. Stacking them into a haphazard pile, he hid them in one of the empty drawers. He gathered more papers off his desk, except for anything which dealt with construction, and added them to another empty drawer. He tidied the rest of his desk a little. Elise knocked on the door.

"Yes. Come in, please." He dropped in his chair and pushed back his hair with fingers to some semblance of order.

The door opened and Elise smiled. "Samuel Ashford, I would like you to meet Sullivan Tarleton, owner of Tarleton Carpentry & Construction," she introduced.

A six-foot-plus male entered the office, his dark blond hair highlighted from the sun, his skin burnished golden from the rays. He was comfortably dressed in stone khakis and a pale blue linen shirt with his company's logo embroidered on the pocket. He carried a steel gray clipboard storage case in one hand. When he lifted the glasses back into his hair, he revealed a pair of warm green eyes.

Samuel rose to his feet and held out his hand. "Hello and thank you for coming so soon, Mr Tarleton."

"Sully, please, and I couldn't wait to get my hands on this old girl. She deserves to be brought back to her original beauty with a few extras." Sully shook hands with Samuel in a firm, but not overdone handshake.

"Call me Samuel. You came highly recommended from Dakota. He couldn't stop mentioning you and your work around here."

"That's Kota for you. He's loyal to locals and friends. How are you two getting along?"

"We're butting heads, but we're getting there. I admit I do admire how the man can cook a meal and this tea... I'm in love with the tea."

Sully chuckled as he settled in the chair when Samuel waved him to it. "Yeah, I enjoy the good meals here in lieu of payments. The tea is one of my favorites."

"Would you like a glass? I have an extra one here and a full pitcher. I've been getting one delivered for the last few days since I kept bugging them for another glass. Dakota snagged a pitcher and filled it instead of a glass."

"Please. The sun is out strong today and this is the first time I've got to stay inside for longer than five minutes."

"I'm going nuts with the heat. I came from New York and prefer air conditioning." Samuel poured a glass and set it in front of Sully.

"This must be a big change for you."

"First day was horrible, plus I was in a full suit, something Dakota talked me out of wearing. He had some of the staff pick up some casual clothes as a welcome gift for me. Apparently, I don't wear enough shorts to their satisfaction." Samuel picked up the glass and enjoyed several swallows.

"He does insist on the casual wear. When it gets deeper into summer, most employees will change over to shorts and matching T-shirts."

"It's the reason you're here. Have you walked through the exterior and interior other than the restaurant?" Samuel scratched at his throat and coughed. "Hmm. Excuse me."

"I did a walk-through on my own about three months ago to send in a package and bid to Edward, but I never got an answer." Sully opened his storage case across his lap and pulled out a simple green folder. "Here is what I collated and what, as someone in the construction field, would look at and be concerned. These are all suggestions, of course."

"Of course." Reaching for the folder, Samuel opened it on his desk. Taking another drink, he scratched his throat again. He cleared it again and shook his head.

"Are you all right?"

"I think something went down..." Samuel cleared his throat.

"You sound a little hoarse, like you got a frog in your throat."

Samuel pressed a hand around his throat as the tightness worsened. He found it harder to breathe. He wheezed louder.

"Samuel..." Sully rose and went around the desk.

"Can't...breathe... Something with tea...strange... Allergy..." Samuel waved a hand as his wheezing increased. "But nuts, not tea..."

"Shit. Damn. Shit..." Sully moved to the doorway. "Dakota! Get your ass in here!" He returned to the desk and dialed nine-one-one.

Dakota raced into the office. "What the hell...? Holy... Samuel, what happened? Are you having a reaction to something? Talk to me."

"Itchy throat. Can't breathe... Swollen..." Samuel fluttered a hand over his chest. His eyes were wide as he met Dakota's gaze. His body was in anaphylactic reaction. How could it have happened? He hadn't had or touched nuts. He stared at the pitcher. "Drink..." He wheezed several times, his breath whistling. Coughing to open his lungs, he felt his tongue swell while his skin itched.

"Where's your EpiPen? Where is it? Are you calling for an ambulance, Sully?" Dakota rushed over to Samuel and patted him down for the small injection pen. He found it in his hip pocket and yanked it out.

"Yeah, I got them on the phone." Sully turned his attention to the operator. "We need an ambulance STAT to the Southern Charm. We have a young man who is having an anaphylactic reaction. We're administering an EpiPen injection. We need to transport him to the hospital ASAP."

"I want him to go to a hospital in Pensacola, not the clinic here," Dakota said.

Sully relayed the request and details.

Samuel wheezed as he stared at Dakota and the pen. His throat swollen and sore, his heart raced as his anxiety increased.

"Easy, Samuel, I'm going to take care of you." Dakota moved the chair and jabbed the orange end of the pen against the middle of Samuel's outer thigh. The auto-injector went through the shorts and into his muscle. He rubbed Samuel's chest in smooth circles. "Breathe with me. Nice and easy. The medicine is going in now. You need to calm down your breathing."

Samuel kept his gaze locked on Dakota's eyes. Dakota picked up Samuel's hand and pressed his fingers against Dakota's chest.

"Follow my breathing, Samuel, keep your eyes on me," Dakota said.

Wiggling his fingers against Dakota's hand, Samuel concentrated on how Dakota's strong chest expanded, feeling his muscles move with every breath. He tried to swallow but coughed.

"Don't rush yourself. Sully, I need a clean glass of water. Can you get it?" Dakota asked, not looking away from Samuel.

"I got it," Sully said and raced out of the room.

"The medicine is almost in, Samuel. We're at eight... Nine... Ten." Dakota finished counting to hold the injector in place. When it was empty, he removed the pen and put it back in the case. He stretched out and hit the intercom button on the desk phone.

"Elise here."

"Elise, we have an incoming Sheriff and EMTs. Bring them back to Samuel's office ASAP."

"Oh my God... What happened?"

"Samuel is having an anaphylactic reaction and needs transport to the hospital. I'm going with him. Just bring them back here as soon as they arrive."

"Yes, Chef."

Dakota rubbed a thumb in circles on Samuel's chest. "You're doing great. Keep breathing with me."

Samuel kept his fingers against Dakota's chest.

Dakota lifted the case into Samuel's view. "There's one dosage left in here." He glanced at the pen. "Do you have another?"

Samuel shook his head. He gripped Dakota's hand.

"Okay." Dakota squeezed Samuel's fingers in reassurance. "I'm not going anywhere. I promise. Let's keep you calm and breathing."

"Here's a glass of water," Sully said as he rushed back in, holding a glass with a straw.

"Let's see if you can take a sip." Dakota took the glass and held the straw to Samuel's lips with his free hand.

Samuel shook his head and wheezed. He couldn't get anything past his throat, barely able to breathe while he waited for the medicine to work.

"Okay. It's okay. I thought to give it a try." Dakota set the glass aside.

"Ambulance is on its way. We'll get you to the hospital," Sully said.

"I alerted Elise."

"Shit, I should have buzzed her," Sully said. "What set this off for him? He isn't allergic to tea. He said something about nuts."

"He's allergic to all kinds of nuts."

Sully looked around the desk and office. "I don't see anything to set him off around here."

"I know. Since he told me about the allergy, I made sure all the products with nuts separated even farther than what I have to protect any restaurant visitor. Where the hell did the damn nuts get in? How could you ingest it without knowing, Samuel?" Dakota slammed a fist against the desk with a burst of anger. "I'm damn careful in my kitchen. I pride myself on no patron having any kind of food allergy trouble within my kitchen." Dakota flexed his fingers before he tilted the chair back to help Samuel relax and continue to breathe. "When did this start? Did you see his reaction begin?"

"Yeah, I saw him scratch his throat, clear it a few times, but I didn't really think anything of it. I thought he was nervous meeting me," Sully said.

"When did it start?"

Sully pulled his eyebrows together. He glanced at Samuel, who managed to lift a hand and point it to something on his desk. Samuel made a drinking motion with his hand.

"The tea! His reaction came after drinking the tea," Sully said as he lifted the glass. He sniffed once, his eyebrows pulled together, and he sniffed again. "What the hell...?"

"What? What is it?"

Sully stuck the glass in Dakota's face. "Take a sniff. Tell me what you smell."

Dakota took the glass and took a long sniff. His face blanched. "Almonds. I smell almonds." Dakota picked up the pitcher and he caught the same distinctive scent. He paced in front of the desk, his hand clenched at his side. "Sonofabitch..." He stopped and dropped back to Samuel's side. He drew his fingers through

Samuel's hair. He leaned closer and pressed a gentle kiss to Samuel's forehead. "I'm sorry. I'm so damn sorry."

Samuel tried to smile and reassure him, but couldn't get words passed his tight throat.

"No, no, it isn't, not when you're suffering." Dakota shook his head and looked at Sully. "Is the Sheriff coming with the ambulance? Someone tried to poison him to cause this reaction."

Sully watched the gentle interaction between them. He cleared his throat and nodded. "Yeah, he's on his way. He'll lead the ambulance to us."

Samuel shook his head, exhausted from the reaction and shock.

"Ssh. We'll handle it. You keep working on your breathing," Dakota said as he helped Samuel unbutton the top buttons to release some of the tension from the swelling. "I'm so sorry someone did this to you."

Samuel shrugged a shoulder.

"What is going on around here?" Malcolm entered the room and closed the door.

"Someone slipped almonds in the iced tea. I'm thinking it's one of the liquid forms," Dakota said with a growl of anger. He held out the pitcher to let Malcolm sniff the evidence.

"But he's…" Malcolm looked at Samuel. "Allergic… Bad. Holy shit. What do you want me to do, Chef?" Mal asked, being formal with the request.

"I want you in the kitchen and to look at everything and everyone. I want to know how the hell this happened. The Sheriff will be here so you can work with him," Dakota ordered.

"Will do, Chef. Samuel, I'm so sorry this happened," Malcolm said.

Samuel leaned against Dakota's shoulder, exhausted.

Dakota caressed his hand down Samuel's hair. "Keep the pitcher here for evidence until the Sheriff can examine it."

"Yes, Chef," Malcolm said and moved out of the office. "Paramedics are here." He waved a hand to direct them. "In here. He's in here."

"Thanks," someone called and two men in pale blue uniforms with red crosses entered the office. They carried multiple packs of gear and a body brace. "Hey there, I'm Gray. What's going on here?"

"This is Samuel. He has a nut allergy with a strong anaphylactic reaction. I gave him the dosage from his EpiPen and have been trying to get him relaxed and to concentrate on breathing. He can't take a sip of water, though," Dakota said and moved his hand to Samuel's shoulder.

"Hey, Samuel, can I listen to your breathing?" Gray said as he pulled out a stethoscope and a few tools.

Samuel nodded and opened his mouth, but closed it.

"You can't talk right now, I understand. Just worry about staying calm and relax," Gray said as he moved his stethoscope over Samuel's chest to listen to his heart rate and breathing. "You're a little swollen in the throat and mouth area."

Samuel licked his lips.

"Can't get any moisture moved around," Gray said and nodded. "Okay. Let's load you up and get you to the hospital."

"Can I go with him?" Dakota asked.

"Who are you?"

"I'm Dakota."

"Are you his partner?"

"Yes," Dakota said, squeezing Samuel's hand.

"Sure. I'll make room in the back." Gray motioned to the other paramedic. "Hey, Norman, bring the stretcher in here. I don't want to lay him back and chance his throat closing up on us."

"You got it," Norman said. He returned with a gurney. He lowered it closer to the ground.

"Okay. Dakota and you, cute fella..." Gray pointed to Sully.

"Me? I'm Sully," Sully said with a grin. "I'm a friend."

"Okay. I need both of you to help me move Samuel slow and steady from the chair to the gurney. Samuel, don't move unless I deem it necessary," Gray said and moved Dakota and Sully to the positions he wanted. "Norman, hold onto the gurney. We move on three..." He began the simple countdown and everyone moved.

Within a few minutes, Samuel and Dakota were in the back of the ambulance with Gray. Norman climbed in the front and drove them away with sirens wailing. Gray concentrated on helping Samuel to stabilize throughout the ride to the hospital. The entire time, Dakota kept hold of one of Samuel's hands between his.

Chapter Fifteen

When Samuel's levels refused to stabilize with additional help, the doctor decided to keep him in overnight. Samuel banged his head a couple of times against the flat pillow.

"All I need is return to the Charm and relax," Samuel said.

"I'm sorry, Mr Ashford, but not with your oxygen levels low and your heart rate high. The combination isn't good. I want to keep you overnight and assess your condition. In the morning, if all goes well, I'll release you," Doctor Elliott Sheffield said as he adjusted his stethoscope.

"And if I want to leave now?"

"It'll be without my consent and approval. I don't recommend the option."

Dakota clasped Samuel's hand in an apparent attempt to stop him from arguing. "Listen to the doc. Take the night to get yourself better."

"Okay. Okay. Fine." Samuel closed his eyes and thumped his head again.

"Hey, stop, it won't be so bad." Dakota placed a gentle kiss on Samuel's forehead. With his thumb, he stroked circles around the back of Samuel's hand. "When will he be moved?"

"I have a nurse checking the available beds now, but I suspect within the next hour or so he'll go upstairs," Doctor Sheffield said.

"Call Sully and go back to the Charm. They need you for the rib-dinner rush. It's the big night you promoted for the ribs. You can't miss it. Dorian told me how it'll be a madhouse," Samuel said.

"No. I'm staying with you," Dakota said.

"You can't do anything to help right now. I mean it, return to the Charm and help them get through the night. Call Sully to pick you up. I need to reschedule my meeting with him." Samuel squeezed Dakota's hand back.

"I'll come back after dinner and stay with you." Dakota glared at the doctor. "I will be allowed to stay the night with him?"

"I'll make a note in the file to give you access, but I shouldn't see a problem with your request around regular visiting hours. Let me go and check on a room. You can have a few more moments together." With a smile, the doctor left them in the fabric cubicle.

"I don't want to stay here," Samuel said. "Bust me outta here."

"Nope. No can do."

"Shit…"

"What happened? Do you have any idea?"

"Dorian came in and gave me a fresh pitcher of tea. We talked about how good the ribs smelled and he explained how the event would happen. He returned to the kitchen and Elise notified me Sully had arrived. I did a quick cleaning of the office," Samuel said.

"It doesn't make any sense about Dorian. He loves the Charm and the whole crew. He wouldn't do anything so cruel, it's not in him."

"I'm not putting any blame on him either. I don't know who poured the tea. After I sipped from the glass a few times, my throat became itchy and my tongue swelled. From there it got worse."

"The almond essence was definitely in the liquid. I'm sure of it." Dakota paced next to Samuel's gurney. "Who would want to hurt you? Who knows about your allergy?"

"Malcolm and Dorian were the closest when you asked if I had any allergies, but there were other kitchen employees. There could have been housekeeping staff in the hallway..." Samuel trailed off and stopped.

Stopping, Dakota faced him. "What? What is it?"

"That waiter... Allan... He stopped and listened to our conversation. I saw him behind you. He knew about my reaction."

"Nah... Couldn't be. He's a little odd, but not dangerous."

"Dakota, he hates me more than anyone. Anytime I pass him, I feel like he wants to shoot daggers into my back for being near you."

"Come on..."

"Don't count him out. Please. I don't know of anyone else."

Shoving hands through his hair, Dakota grumbled. "I hate mysteries, especially within my kitchen. I'll get to the bottom of it. I promise. I need to speak with the Sheriff and tell him about what you said."

"Yes, go ahead and talk to him. I'm sure he'll want to talk to me."

"He's a good guy, the Sheriff, a top-notch friend. I trust him."

"Good to know."

Someone cleared their throat to interrupt the conversation. Doctor Sheffield stood in the opened curtain, hand clasped over the metal clipboard. "Sorry to interrupt, but a room is being prepared for Samuel and instructions placed with the nursing station to allow you and others to visit, Mr Mitchell."

"Dakota, please," Dakota said. "Thanks for setting it up."

"No one should be alone when in a hospital if they have loved ones, no matter the sex or partnership."

"Thanks again. I'll see you tonight." Dakota rose and braced one hand on the mattress next to. Samuel's far side. "Okay?"

"I'll be fine. See you tonight. Could you bring my..."

"No. No electronics." Dakota shook his head with an amused look upon his face. "You're going to rest tonight. I'll tell Sully to come back to the Charm tomorrow for your meeting."

"But...I'll be bored."

"Too bad. No work. You can sleep or watch TV." Dakota tilted farther down and placed his lips against Samuel's in a soft, tender lip lock.

Samuel lifted his hand to hold onto Dakota's shoulder as he slid deeper into the kiss. *God, this man knows how to kiss.* He moaned soft.

Dakota pulled back and grinned. "We'll explore more later. Rest." He gave him another kiss, straightened, then nodded to the doctor. "Take good care of him. Please."

"He'll have the best of care," the doctor said with a brisk nod.

Dakota walked out of the cubicle as he pulled out his phone.

"Where can I get one of those fellas for myself?" Doctor Sheffield asked. His green eyes sparkled underneath his dark lashes.

"I don't know, but I'm surprised I got him," Samuel said with an answering snicker. He wished he was heading back with Dakota, instead of being stuck in this stupid hospital gown.

"Oh well. Guess I gotta keep looking. Hard to find a good gay guy who's single and caring." The doctor shook his head. "Let me go check on your room."

"Thanks, Doc, perhaps you should visit Shore Breeze. Maybe you can find someone while there."

"Sounds like a good idea. Is there a medical clinic in town that could use a hand? I've been thinking about leaving the hospital for a quieter practice."

"I'm sure there is, I haven't explored the entire town. You should ask Dakota. He's lived there for a long time."

"Perhaps. Try to get some rest. We'll move you to a room in a bit." The doctor walked away. He twitched the curtains closed behind him.

Samuel closed his eyes to remember the kiss and look in Dakota's eyes as he slipped into a nap. Though the doctor was pretty darn good-looking, his eyes had stayed on Dakota the entire time. The chef was the man for him, something he had proven the last few nights they'd spent together, their bodies tangled and sweaty.

* * * *

Pulling in front of the Charm in Sully's truck, Dakota opened the door and climbed down. He stared at the Charm, his home and life, and wondered who inside had wanted to try to kill Samuel. Sure, he'd first thought that Samuel was only here to ruin his home, destroy everything he loved about it, but within the first week of Samuel being here he'd changed his mind. No one had ever bothered to join him on his morning trips to town and learn what he did, not even a lover.

Samuel insisted on being with him, learning everything he could about the Charm. When Samuel had shown him the changes he wanted to make, pointed the issues to him so he could see them in a different way, Dakota had understood. Samuel wanted to help make the Charm better, stronger, and bring more visitors to keep everyone working. He knew everything had shifted after the morning shopping. When they'd spent the rest of the morning together in Samuel's bed, learning each other's bodies in the best way possible. He couldn't give him up.

Dakota shoved a hand through his hair.

"Hey, are you doing okay?" Sully asked as he stopped next to Dakota.

"Yeah, thanks for the ride home. Who the hell would do such a thing? Don't they know Samuel and his family are probably our last hope in keeping the Charm open and running? I... Shit... I looked into things and it hit me. It hit me hard." Dakota rubbed a hand over his chest. "I could lose everything I built within six months if we don't turn things around. We need the Ashfords and the capital they bring to the table."

"Did you tell this to Samuel?"

"It hit me after seeing him struggle for breath, injured by something which came from my kitchen."

"Have you kissed him?"

"Yeah, there were sparks... Damn, they're there when I'm with him."

"A petit New Yorker conquers the Southern playboy chef." Sully bumped a fist against Dakota's shoulder. "Glad I got to see it happen."

"Goofball," Dakota said and stepped forward to the old antebellum home. He didn't tell Sully he'd done more than kiss the petite New Yorker. A tall figure stepped out on the sagging porch. He recognized the clothing and nodded to him. "Hello, Sheriff."

"Dakota, it's good to see you. How is Mr Ashford?" Sheriff Robin Burke, head of the local precinct office of the Escambia County Sheriff's Office, asked. He shifted and stood in a strong stance. His fingers hooked around his utility belt.

"The doctor is keeping him under observation since he isn't stabilized," Dakota said. "I left to take care of the dinner crowd and I'll return to the hospital. Am I allowed to operate the kitchen?"

"Yes. I called one of my investigators in and he collected the evidence we need. Malcolm helped locate the areas which would be interesting to us. It saved some time. Both of us spoke with various employees about what happened. Did Mr Ashford tell you anything about what happened?"

"Yeah, we managed to talk."

"Tell me your side of things," Sheriff Burke said as he pulled out a leather-bound pad and pen. He flipped the pad open as Dakota relayed everything Samuel had said to him. "Okay. I need to keep pulling things together, but I'll get back to you."

"Do we need to keep any eye on anything? What am I supposed to do? Keep a watch over everyone?"

"I would suggest caution, additional inspection of food items, but I'll take care of the other matters. You take care of the Charm and Mr Ashford."

"Sheriff..." Dakota sighed. "Robin, please, we've been friends a damn long time."

"As a friend, I want to tell you more. As a law officer, I can't speak about an ongoing investigation."

Dakota opened his mouth to protest, but stopped when Robin held up a hand and shook his head.

"I can't, Dakota."

"All right. I understand."

"I'll need to speak with Mr Ashford, when he's able to talk, to confirm what he said to you and additional questions."

"He should be released tomorrow. I was planning on bringing him home, I mean back to the Charm, after my morning buys."

"No, you were right the first way. You want to bring him home," Robin said with a smile. "Seems you found someone to learn to adore and love."

"Perhaps, I don't know what I have."

Robin glanced at Sully and nodded to him. "He's hooked."

"Like a dangling fish on a worm, only he doesn't realize he's taken," Sully said and clapped a hand against Dakota's shoulder, knocking him forward a step.

"Ow. What the hell...?" Dakota looked between them. "I have a rib dinner rush to prepare for if I'm allowed in my kitchen."

"The kitchen is cleared. We took a few things. Malcolm has the list of items we took for forensics testing. We'll return them once cleared," Robin said.

"What—"

Robin held up a hand and shook his head.

"Shit, Robin."

"When I learn more and speak with Mr Ashford, I can discuss the investigation. Okay?"

Dakota blew out a long breath and nodded.

"I'll stop in tomorrow and speak with Mr Ashford. Enjoy your evening, fellas, wish I could have a plate of those ribs," Robin said before he stepped down and went off to the marked vehicle. He put on a dark Stetson, waved a hand out of the window and drove away.

"This is so messed up," Dakota said, leaning his head back and staring at the sky.

Sully bumped his shoulder again. "Concentrate on food and Samuel for now. Let Robin handle the rest."

"It was someone in my employ. Someone in my building dared to strike against another person and cause deliberate harm. Who the hell would do this?"

"I don't know, buddy. Give Robin time to do what he needs. Now, go do what you do best. Cook."

"Thanks, Sully. Come back tomorrow and speak with Samuel. He does have wonderful ideas. I want you to be the one to work on this place. You know her issues, her charms so to speak."

"You couldn't keep me away even with several rows of barbed wire wrapped around this place. I'll agree to what he wishes. I saw the list of suggestions and there are others to add. I'll be here. I'm not missing this chance."

"We need to keep this place going. Bring her back to her grace and pride."

"We will."

"Find Reece if you can and let him know we'll need his skills," Dakota said and held up his fist.

Sully bumped knuckles. "I'll do it. See you tomorrow."

Dakota turned to head back into the Charm, ready to do what he did every night. Create delicious food and feed people, something he loved—only part of him wouldn't be in the kitchen. He left his heart behind in the hospital.

Chapter Sixteen

After yet another check on his condition and poking by another nurse, Samuel opened his eyes and looked around the darkened room. Something warm pressed against his arm and he turned to the side. His jaw dropped.

Samuel found Dakota stretched out on the reclining chair. He was fast asleep with a light blanket thrown over his legs. He kept one hand on the bed and one on Samuel's arm.

Dakota opened his eyes, stretched and twisted his shoulders, then lifted his mouth in a half smile. "Hey there. How are you doing?"

"I'm tired of being poked and prodded."

"A few more hours and you'll be sprung free," Dakota said, stroking his fingers across Samuel's skin.

Samuel's cock responded to the gentle touch and he moaned. "I'm glad you're here. I can't believe the change between us. All last week, I thought you hated the idea of my being within your beloved Charm. Somehow things changed. You kissed me, kept watch over me and touched me like you want more. What happened?"

Dakota dropped the recliner and leaned closer to the bed. "Within these last few days, I noticed how much you care for the Charm. You want to help rebuild her back to her glory, save her from ruin and help the town. You want what I want. To save the Charm."

"Is this the only reason for your change of heart? Did you take me into your bed because you didn't want me to give up on the Charm?"

"The Charm is my life, my heart, Samuel."

"You'll tolerate me only because I can save the Charm for you?"

"No… It isn't what I mean," Dakota said.

Samuel closed his eyes and turned away from him.

"Samuel, you're not listening. Please. Let me explain," Dakota said, clenching his fingers around Samuel's wrist.

"Unbelievable. I can't believe I fell into bed with you." Samuel tugged his wrist free. "You need to leave now. I need to sleep. Send someone to pick me up in the morning when I'm released, please." He closed his eyes and shifted on the uncomfortable bed to put his back toward Dakota.

"I'm not leaving."

"I don't want you here." Samuel kept his eyes closed tight.

"Sonofa… This isn't how I want things to go," Dakota said.

The bed shifted underneath him. Samuel saw Dakota sliding onto the bed.

"What are you doing?"

"I'm trying to fit on this damn bed to hold you. There are times I hate being over six-feet." Dakota managed to spoon against Samuel's resisting body. He wrapped an arm around Samuel's waist and tugged him closer. "I want to hold you like I did during our first morning together. It was our first time being true to ourselves and our desires."

"I don't..."

"Shut up," Dakota said as he tilted Samuel's face to plant a long kiss on his lips. When he pulled back, he stared at him. "I want you. You for who you are and not for what you're doing for a building. I've wanted you the first moment we ran into each other and tangled limbs on the floor."

"This isn't what you said earlier."

"I didn't explain myself right. Hell, I just woke up and you know I work better with food than words or people. Let me get my brains scrambled back together without the benefit of coffee. I've been worried like hell over you." Dakota kissed his temple again. He drifted his hand across Samuel's chest and belly.

"If you're playing with my head, I'm going to beat you stupid. You better know I'm not an easy score."

"I wouldn't take you to be an easy score. Not here, not now, and not like this. Though, there is one advantage."

"What?"

"Your ass is so darn available to me right now by hanging out of this ridiculous gown."

"Hey." Samuel smacked Dakota's hip.

"Did I ever mention how much I like your bubble ass? It's a cute round butt." Dakota slid a hand between them until he could cup the available flesh.

"You're unbelievable." Samuel moaned when one of Dakota's fingers slid between his cheeks. "What are you...? We're in a freaking hospital room. Besides, you said I'm too loud for a public tryst."

"I also said I could occupy your mouth so you wouldn't be noisy." Dakota tugged the gown from Samuel's neck. He nibbled on Samuel's earlobe, found a sensitive spot against the ear, and made his way down the length of Samuel's neck. He licked and marked the skin. He pressed his face against the curve between Samuel's neck and shoulder. He nipped on the corded muscle connecting them. At the same time, he rimmed Samuel's opening with his fingers. "I want to touch you."

"You can't, we shouldn't do this here." Samuel swallowed. "Don't..." He swallowed again. "Don't tease me like this."

"Do you not want my touch? You couldn't stop touching me every night this last week."

"You better not want to touch me because I'm here to help you keep your precious building or for the damn Ashford money."

Dakota stopped his fingers and moved Samuel onto his back. Samuel stared at Dakota. The soft lights of the various machines and the lowered light over his bed illuminated the highlights in Dakota's hair. His heart rate machine beeped as his rate accelerated while the silence between them extended.

"Why have you never talked to me about this? Did someone do this to you? Use you because of your work or family money? Did some man try...?"

"Tried and accomplished," Samuel said in a soft tone covered in bitterness hidden within his heart. "I wanted to forget about it in your arms."

"I brought the hurt back with a stupid side remark. Shit, I'm an ass." Dakota dropped his head and shook it. "How did this happen?"

"It's the usual way. He knew who I was and I didn't know his game, but fell for his looks. He didn't want me, just my money and a position in my family's company." Samuel shrugged and looked away.

Dakota placed a finger against his chin and gently forced him back. "I'm not here because of your name or money. I'm staying because I'm holding you in my arms and no one else."

"I'm from the family who purchased the Charm and is saving it."

"You didn't have to save it. You mentioned how you fought with your father to save her. When I know you could have taken one look at her, called your family to discuss the problems, tell them and us to forget it, and sent the order to shut down the B&B side. You wouldn't get the restaurant, since I own it, but I couldn't fight for the Charm."

"The moment I saw her, there's no way I could give up on her."

"You saw the potential in her old grace. You wanted to learn about her, me and everything else in our little town."

"Did all this make you want to jump me? You are one strange man."

"It wasn't a factor the morning I followed you upstairs instead of going for a morning run." Dakota touched his fingers to Samuel's chest, above his heart.

"What made you follow me?"

"I followed you because you cared about what I do, where I go, and about me as a person as well as a chef. You're the first one to join me on my morning errands. No one else ever gave a damn to wake up and walk around with me."

"Following you around at four a.m. is part of my job to understand all the details in running the Charm and restaurant."

"It wasn't the only reason you went with me."

"Well, no, I was damn intrigued by everything you do."

"Same here." Dakota tugged on the gown until he could kiss Samuel's shoulder. "I followed you because of your heart and your caring for a place you didn't know and for people who are complete strangers. I don't want anything to do with the corporation. I only want the son. I want you because you're Samuel. Not Sam. Not Sammy. Samuel." Dakota kissed him, another warm lip lock, flicked his tongue against Samuel's lower lip. He shifted until they were spooned again. Only this time, he twitched the gown to cover Samuel's ass.

"What are you doing?"

"It's late and you need sleep. When I get you back home, I'm spending an entire night making love with you." Dakota kissed his neck.

"What…"

"Sleep. I'll hold you as you sleep and heal," Dakota whispered.

With the firm press of Dakota's cock against his ass, his heavy arm around his waist, and Dakota's warm breath teasing the hairs on his cheek, Samuel had never felt safer. Something had changed in the man who held him. Something deep and strong and he wanted to know more about this change. It was a change since their first afternoon, something more distinct and…permanent? He could only hope. Did Dakota want something more than a simple fuck buddy type of relationship? He let out a long breath, he hadn't realized he'd been holding, closed his eyes, and slowly fell asleep.

* * * *

Hours later, Samuel woke again when something shifted behind him. He blinked and glanced over his shoulder to see Dakota rising and pulling on a shirt. "Where are you going?"

"I need to get to the markets and make purchases for the Charm. Soon as I'm done, I'll be back to help break you out of this place. Give me an hour or more, but I'll be here," Dakota said and leaned in to kiss Samuel's mouth.

"Don't leave," Samuel said in a soft tone.

"What?"

"Don't go... You got everything for the rest of the weekend's meals. Right? So there's no need for you to leave for the markets. Please."

"I left all of the other mornings and came back to your bed."

"It's different. Don't leave."

Tilting his head, Dakota sat on the edge of the bed.

"Please. Think about what's in your pantry and coolers. You can make anything out of what you have."

"What's wrong? Why do you not want me to leave?"

"For once, I want to come first to someone. Not because of a job, money, family, nothing but me. Is it selfish to want to be the first thought on someone's mind for once in my life?"

"Samuel, you know I'm a chef. I've been doing this all week. I need to do this every morning to have the fresh supplies to create meals."

"No, there's no reason for you to go out every single morning. You don't have to. You can make bigger buys twice a week to cover everything and pick up something special here and there. You'll save more money and time."

Dakota pulled his eyebrows together.

"You can work with the various markets to set up the timing."

"How do you know this? When did you think about these options?"

"I figured it out after seeing what you go through every morning leaving our bed. In between all the calls I was making, I worked on the ideas. I'll show you all the figures when we get back to the Charm."

Dakota tilted his head. "You figured all this out for me?"

"I wanted to see if there was a way to take some stress out of your mornings. Plus, I hated being left alone in bed and don't want you to leave a warm lover. I figured if this works it could give you more time and sleep so you can continue to do what you love. You can still go for a morning run and swim, but not so early." Samuel lifted the sheet to invite Dakota back.

"Let me send a text or two and explain to Frank and the others," Dakota said as he reached out and picked up his phone from the table. Receiving confirmations from his contacts, he placed the phone down. He kicked off his shoes and pulled off his shirt. "You're a brilliant handsome man. Thank you for trying to figure all this out. I hope it does work." He kissed Samuel before he snuggled them back together.

"I wish I told you this earlier in the week, but I wanted to gather the information first." Samuel yawned, closed his eyes once more, a smile upon his lips.

"Go back to sleep. I'm not leaving until the doctor springs you."

"Hmm, he is cute."

Dakota goosed his ass and caused him to yelp. "Brat. Sleep."

Samuel grinned, wiggled back against him and fell asleep. *Perhaps things will be better from here on out.* At least once they figured out who slipped him nuts.

* * * *

Bright sunlight poured into the room and hit his eyes. Groaning and turning his head, Samuel opened his eyes and woke up. He didn't feel a strong, warm body against him. "Dakota?"

"Here I am. I needed coffee," Dakota said.

"You're not here with me," Samuel said as he turned his head and looked at him.

"I didn't want to disturb your sleep by climbing back in and I'm too damn big for both of us to be comfortable," Dakota said as he relaxed in his chair, sipping on a cup of coffee.

"Hmm, coffee smells good," Samuel said.

"Soon as you get clearance to go, I'll get you a cup. Okay?"

Samuel nodded and raised the bed to a sitting position. "Anyone come by yet?"

"The nurse stepped in to check your morning info. I asked about the doctor and she mentioned he'll be here in around another hour," Dakota said with a yawn and stretch.

There was a knock on the door and it opened. "Good morning, Mr Ashford, how are you feeling this morning?" The young doctor stepped into the room with a smile on his face. He nodded to Dakota as he made his way to the bed. He lifted the clipboard and flipped through the various notations the nurses had made over the last few hours.

"Morning, Doc. Sheffield. Can I leave?" Samuel asked instead of answering his inquiry.

The doctor chuckled and lowered the clipboard. "Your numbers stabilized, there's no more swelling or reaction, and your breathing is stronger. So, yes, you can have permission to leave. Here is the refill capsule for your EpiPen and a prescription for refills as needed. I upped the dosage another level to help you react faster." He pulled out a package from a pocket and placed it on the bed.

Samuel took the white bag and opened it to see the box. "The refill script is inside?"

"Yes." The doctor scribbled something on the chart. "I'll have the nurses prepare your release papers. A nurse will come in, unhook all the electrodes, stop and remove your IV and bandage you up. You can get ready to leave afterwards."

"Thanks, Doc. Sheffield, I appreciate it," Samuel said.

"You're welcome. I hope I can visit Shore Breeze on my next set of days off. Otherwise, I don't want to see you back here. Stay away from those nuts, okay?"

"I'll do my best to keep our distance," Samuel said and held out his hand.

The doctor leaned over and shook Samuel's hand. He turned to Dakota and they shook hands. "It was a pleasure to meet you, Dakota. I hope to check out your restaurant and enjoy your food."

"We'll keep a table and room at the Charm ready for you, Doctor Sheffield," Dakota said. "Thank you for taking good care of him."

"I didn't do much, helped his body acclimate and heal." The doctor shrugged and grinned before he waved goodbye and stepped out of the room.

"He's a nice guy," Samuel said. "Do we have a clinic in Shore Breeze?"

"It's a mid-sized, multi-service clinic, but needs some work and updates. It's good for minor emergencies and general healthcare. Perhaps they could use a new doctor to oversee the place," Dakota said.

The nurse entered and stopped their conversation. They concentrated on getting Samuel out of the hospital.

Chapter Seventeen

While Dakota drove home, Samuel enjoyed the breeze through his hair and against his face. He craved a shower and time in a soft bed without someone poking and prodding him every couple of hours.

"Hey, sleepy head, we're back. Time to get up," Dakota said as he nudged Samuel's shoulder.

Blinking open his eyes, Samuel realized that he'd fallen asleep at some point. He lifted his head from the doorframe and rubbed his face. "Sorry, I didn't mean to conk out on you."

"You're still recovering, no need to apologize." Dakota gave him a warm smile. "How are you doing?"

"I'll be better when I can take a shower. Are you going to carry me upstairs?" Samuel stretched, twisted to release some pressure in his back then shifted his shoulders a little. He stopped when he glanced down, noticing the telltale bulge under Dakota's zipper, then looked back at Dakota's face.

"It's there. It happens. I'm not excusing it. It happens a lot whenever I'm near you. I watched you sleep and you're quite cute when you're asleep. Though I want to take advantage of it with you, now isn't the time."

"Honest. Nice." Samuel winged up an eyebrow. "Are you sure I stopped being an annoying bastard who's taking away your home?"

"When did I ever call you that?"

"Please…"

"Sorry, I've been an ass, but I tried to change my attitude about everything since we spent our morning together. Not to mention, this episode scared the shit out of me. When I saw you pale, gasping for air, with anxiety crawling around you, I flipped inside."

"Do you want more than being simple fuck buddies with me?"

"I do want more than simple sex. Last night, you were sleepy cute and I enjoyed holding you in my arms." Dakota moved his finger around one of Samuel's curls at his forehead. "There was an adorable bubble butt mooning me. I couldn't resist."

"I can't believe you got horny after seeing me in one of those horrible hospital gowns. They are the worst." Samuel wrinkled his nose and forehead and Dakota laughed.

There was a banging on the metal frame next to Samuel startling the living shit out of both of them.

Sully gave them an annoying grin and wave. "Hello."

"You piece of shit, he just go outta the hospital," Dakota snapped.

Samuel slapped the back of his head against Dakota's chest. "I'm fine, don't snap at him. Hey there, Sully, thanks for the help yesterday."

"Please, he doesn't deserve niceties," Dakota said with a glare at his best friend. "It's his polite way to tell us to get the hell out."

Samuel glanced between the two men. "What's the impolite way?"

"If there were doors, I have a tendency to yank them open and laugh my ass off when you fall on yours," Sully said with a grin.

"You didn't," Samuel said.

"He did. Why do you think I keep the doors off?"

Samuel laughed and Sully joined him.

"Yeah, he's such a lovely friend and real considerate of other people's privacy." Dakota flipped his friend the bird.

"You love me. Don't deny it." Sully looked over the Jeep. "When are you going to get rid of this hunk of junk?"

"See. I'm not the only one afraid to get in this car without a current tetanus booster," Samuel said.

Dakota blew a raspberry and climbed out. He walked around to stand next to Sully.

"You'll never change his mind. Even with the doors off, I wondered if you two were gonna get lucky in front of everyone. I didn't want you to over share with us," Sully said.

"Why the hell not?"

Sully stuck a finger in the air. "One. You're out in the open. Eww. No one wants to see your skinny ass while you do it." Sully shuddered and added a second finger. "Two. I'll be damned if someone else gets lucky and I can't."

"Hey. My ass is pretty nice." Dakota patted his ass and stuck it out. "Anyone would want to catch a glimpse of it. Are you sure you don't wanna see it?" Dakota wiggled said posterior in front of Sully.

Samuel tilted his head back and laughed uproariously.

"Besides, I want to know why no cute guy wants to crawl in the back seat of your truck with you. You're quite a peach and a catch. Aww, poor Sully baby," Dakota said as he patted Sully's cheek with his fingers.

Sully smacked Dakota's fingers away with a playful growl. He shoved Dakota's ass out of his way, setting off more laughter from Samuel. "Shut it. Small damn town," Sully grumbled, stepping back and pushing Dakota out of the way so Samuel could climb down.

Samuel nodded in thanks, grabbed the overnight bag Dakota packed for him and jumped down.

Sully slid out of the way when Dakota moved to Samuel's side. "Well, okay, slide right in there, why don'tcha."

Dakota grinned.

"I'm not a toy to be tugged between you," Samuel said and bumped a fist into Dakota's side.

"Ouch..." Dakota rubbed his side in a playful matter.

"How are you, Sully? Thank you for coming back today," Samuel said, turning his attention to the other tall male.

"It's good to see you up and around. It's not a problem. I do want to talk to you about this old place."

"Good, I'm glad you're still interested."

"How are you feeling, Samuel?"

"I'm much better than yesterday. I didn't enjoy spending time in the hospital, but the doctor was cute and interested."

"He isn't getting further with you than a dinner at the restaurant. Nothing else," Dakota said, wiggling a finger in front of Samuel.

"He was more interested in you than me. I'm taken."

Dakota's jaw dropped in surprise.

"Yes. Real smooth, Kota," Sully said as he pushed on Dakota's chin with two fingers to close his mouth.

"Okay." Samuel shook his head at them. "Anyway, I wanted to thank you for getting help for me yesterday. I'm glad you were there when it happened. I don't know what would have happened if I was there alone." Samuel shoved a hand through his hair. "I'm sorry about messing up the meeting."

"It sure as hell wasn't your fault. Someone slipped the damn almond essence into your tea," Dakota said, on the edge of a growl.

"Down boy," Sully said as he dropped a hand on Dakota's shoulder.

Dakota waved a hand between all of them. "They could have killed him."

"But they didn't and I'm better now," Samuel said, his tone calm and quiet.

"Yeah, after you spent a freaking night in the hospital on observation. We need to figure out who did this, why, and what to do about it. Whoever it is, I want to strangle the life out of them," Dakota said.

"I'll have to haul your ass into jail and neither one of us will be happy."

A trim, muscled man leaned against a dark SUV. He wore a Sheriff's brown uniform shirt with taupe epaulets and dark-wash jeans. The uniform was finished with embroidered patches, a name badge with a golden star, and duty belt with the typical gun holster and various leather duty gear holders. The Sheriff wore a pair of kick ass ankle-high brown boots.

Dark mirrored sunglasses covered his face. Strands of ebony hair stuck out underneath the buff colored Stetson.

Samuel blinked, a little in shock at the thought of how this hottie was the local Sheriff. Where was the typical beer belly older man at the end of his career?

Damn, the Sheriff is hot!

This time Dakota placed his finger under Samuel's chin and lifted.

"Was I drooling?" Samuel asked.

"Almost. Don't make me jealous."

"I'm in your bed, not his."

"True, but you're not the first to be bowled over by our Sheriff," Dakota said and shifted to his other hip to lean closer to Samuel. "Hello again, Sheriff, glad you could make it back to see us."

The sheriff nodded and tipped the brim of his Stetson to the group as he wandered over to them. His steps were more like a cowboy's stroll.

Clearing his throat, Dakota looked from Samuel to the sheriff. "Samuel Ashford, I would like to introduce Sheriff Robin Burke. Robin is in charge of the local precinct office of Escambia County Sheriff's Office, which is in Pensacola."

"It's a pleasure to meet you, Mr Ashford. Welcome to Shore Breeze," the sheriff said as he held out his hand.

"Samuel, please, Sheriff, and thank you," Samuel said as they shook hands.

"You're right, Sully, he is a cute one," the sheriff said with a wink to Sully.

Samuel flushed under the wonderful masculine attention.

"Call me Robin or Burke. I answer to both."

"How about calling you a pain-in-the-ass?" Dakota said in a drawl tone.

"How about I put handcuffs on you and shove you in the back of my SUV?" the sheriff said, tilting the brim of his Stetson back to glance over the top of his glasses at Dakota.

"Ooh, the Sheriff is kinky. I'm surprised," Sully joked.

Robin turned to Sully, lowering his glasses to glare at him. "Wanna find out how kinky?"

"Bring it, lawman."

"I'm with Sully," Dakota said, leaning against Sully's shoulder to face Robin together. "You keep threatening to do this to me, but you never follow through. I'm beginning to believe you don't care about me."

"Or me, I feel left out," Sully said.

Samuel looked between them.

"Sometimes I don't know why I stay around a small town," Robin said.

"Could we get to the real reason you're hanging around here? Can you tell us anything about what happened to Samuel?" Dakota dropped a hand to place it against Samuel's lower back.

"You know I can't talk about an ongoing investigation. I told you this yesterday, Dakota. I swung by for another look around and have a talk with Samuel."

"Shit, come on."

Samuel dug his elbow into Dakota's side. "Of course, Sheriff, I always have time to talk to a lawman. Would you like to join me in my office? Am I allowed to go back in there?"

Robin pulled off his glasses. "Yes, you're allowed in there. My investigator and I took what we needed from the scene. I'm sorry about the fingerprint dust, but I believe one of the maids did her best to clean it."

Dakota grumbled but stopped at another elbow poking his side. "Okay. Okay. I'll keep out of it for now."

"Sully, would you mind hanging out with Dakota for a few minutes while I speak with the Sheriff? We can continue our meeting after," Samuel said with a glance at Sully, the conditioning to be polite to everyone around him ingrained in him by his mother since he was a child.

"I don't mind at all," Sully said. "Come on, Dakota, you can feed me while we wait."

"Feed you? Why would I do that?" Dakota protested as Sully snagged his arm and dragged him away.

"Because you want me to put in the lowest bid possible to save your pretty Charm," Sully said with a wink over his shoulder at Samuel.

"Sorry, he's been protective of me since this incident happened." Samuel led Robin into the Charm. He stopped when Elise rushed to hug him silly.

"Oh, you poor sweet darling, how could someone do such a horrible thing? Nothing so cruel ever happened here," Elise said through a sniffle as she hugged him again.

"It'll be okay, Elise, please. I'm going to be fine." He awkwardly patted her shoulder.

Elise stepped back, sniffled again, and cupped his cheek. "You're wonderful. Hello, Sheriff, you take care now with our Samuel. He's here to save all of us. We can't lose him."

Robin tipped his brim. "I will, Miss Elise. Just need to ask Samuel a couple of questions."

"Okay." Elise kissed Samuel's cheek and went back to her position.

Samuel blinked a few times to re-steady himself as they moved to the office. He closed the door after they'd stepped inside. He waved Robin to take a chair. He glanced around the room where it happened. He stared at the spot by the desk where he'd collapsed, gasping for breath.

"Are you okay, Samuel? We can talk somewhere else." Robin removed his hat and watched Samuel.

"I'm okay. Just need to face my fears of what happened in here. I don't want it to happen again."

"I'm going to do my best to make sure it doesn't."

Letting out a breath, Samuel dropped his bag in the corner. He settled in the chair and turned toward the sheriff. He crossed his hands across the desktop. "Well, Sheriff, what would you like to ask me?"

"I need you to take me through everything that happened since you arrived at the Charm to the incident yesterday," Robin said as he pulled out a small notebook and pen.

Samuel nodded, expecting the questioning would begin there. He took a deep breath to steady his nerves and went through his accounts of the last couple of days. At specific points, the Sheriff made him backtrack, as he added in direct questions to fill in gaps and walked him through various sections. Robin took him through the story several times to check his story and timeline.

"It matches with a lot of what I heard from other staff. Dakota told me you suspected one person, a waiter named Allan, who overheard a conversation. Can you fill me in there?"

Samuel shuddered when he remembered the looks the young waiter had sent his way. He told Robin the similar suspicions he shared with Dakota, adding details when Robin asked.

"Thank you for the additional information. This should do it for me," Robin said. He replaced his notepad and pulled out a business card. He set the card on the desk. "Here is my contact info if you remember anything else."

"Is that everything?"

"For now, yes. I'm already following a few leads with my investigator. If we learn more, I'll let you know any updates. Please be careful with everything you ingest or touch. I'm sure Dakota will be doing the same."

"Of course and thank you for returning to speak with me today," Samuel said.

"I'll keep in touch." Rising from the chair, Robin shook hands with Samuel and replaced his Stetson. "Take care and keep watch."

"Thank you, Sheriff," Samuel said and walked him out of the office. He gave a wave as Robin disappeared down the hallway.

"Meeting over?" Dakota asked as he appeared in the kitchen doorway.

"With the Sheriff, it is. He pretty much knew the timeline, just needed me to fill in a few holes and extra information," Samuel said.

"Hopefully it'll help him figure out who the hell did this. I hate not knowing," Dakota said, shoving a hand through his hair.

"You're not the only one. We stay cautious and keep an eye on things." Samuel clapped his hands together and rubbed them. "Sully, how about we continue our meeting in my office? That is if you still have time to speak with me."

"I have another hour I can give you and would like to finish our meeting," Sully said with a grin.

"Good." Samuel glanced at Dakota and saw how the man wanted to say something. "I'll be all right the rest of the day, Dakota. I'm in no danger of a relapse. I know you will guard everything in the kitchen."

Dakota grumbled and shifted a foot back and forth.

"Please. We'll talk tonight after you finish dinner."

Dakota held out his hands. "Are you hungry? We didn't have breakfast. Do you two need anything from the kitchen?"

"Coffee would be great," Samuel said. "I could use the boost."

"Food?"

"One of those delicious chicken salad sandwiches you made the last time would be awesome."

"Sully, sorry I didn't get to feed you the last hour. Want something with Samuel?"

"I'll take the same as him."

"Got it. I'll bring it into the office for you both," Dakota said, before stepping over to Samuel and placing a kiss against his temple. "Don't push yourself too hard. Okay?"

"I know," Samuel said.

"Good." He returned to the kitchen.

"Come on in, again, and let's get talking about how we can fix this place," Samuel said with a grin and wave to Sully.

"Sounds good to me."

Chapter Eighteen

Over two hours, Samuel and Sully discussed everything from the smallest of items to the larger ones including the wrap-around porch. They enjoyed the lunch Dakota provided and argued over price, materials and timing of everything.

"What about the old owner house? Do you want my crew to tear it down?" Sully asked as he leaned back and crossed hands over his flat stomach.

Samuel's eyebrows pulled together as he stared at Sully. "Owner house? What owner house?"

"There's a carriage house which was converted to an owner house at the same time the B&B was altered to its current layout. The original owners lived in the small house instead of on the third floor."

"Really? Where is it? What kind of shape is it in?"

"It's been abandoned for fifty years, give or take some," Sully said with a wiggle of his head as he thought about something. "It's on the other side of the so-called parking space in the overgrown jungle. You can't see it from here."

"Do we have a key? Do we need one?"

"I don't know. How about checking the desk drawers?" Sully suggested.

"I want to see this place. Keys, we need some keys," Samuel said as he pushed back from the desk and dug through the various drawers. He reached all the way in the back of the lap drawer and hit pay dirt. He came up with an old key ring and on it dangled three large keys. "How about these?"

"They could work. Let's go check it out," Sully said as he rose to his feet with Samuel right behind him.

They left the office and were heading down the hall when Dakota stuck his head out of the kitchen.

"Where are you two heading?" he called out.

"To find this owner house Sully mentioned and see what kind of shape it's in," Samuel said, jingling the ring in his hand. "I found keys. Did you know about the house?"

"Only there was one here on the property, but I didn't know about it. Hang on." Dakota disappeared from the opening and reappeared without his apron. "I'm tagging along."

"What about dinner?"

"Everything is ready and it'll be quiet after the craziness of the rib dinner last night. Mal can handle things for a few minutes."

"Okay. Lead the way, Sully. You get to deal with any critters too," Samuel said with a shiver.

"Snakes?"

"Eww..." Samuel said with another shiver.

Sully chuckled as he first rushed over to his black truck. He returned with a flashlight and long scrap of wood. "Don't know how dark it will be and this will help with the critters and jungle. I don't appreciate the slithery ones."

"On to the jungle," Samuel said and pointed at the overgrown disaster surrounding the cleared part of the property. They headed off across the gravel and between two cars. He shook his head and stared at the creeping nature. "This needs to be tamed."

"We'll get Reece on the job," Dakota said.

"We need someone on this mess." Samuel grabbed a thick stick and beat back a few sharp blades of tall grass. "Where are we going to find this mystery house?"

"Just beyond the parking lot and through the woods," Sully said.

"Are we going over a bridge?" Samuel quipped.

Sully laughed.

Dakota glanced at him with a raised eyebrow.

"What? It fits." Samuel motioned a hand around the tangled mess. "As long as we don't find a wolf in grandma's clothing on the other side—I don't know if I can handle a wolf right now."

Dakota shook his head.

The adventure took a few more minutes of batting down the grass, overgrown bushes, dangling Spanish moss and fallen logs but they made it through. They all stood in front of a smaller version of the Charm.

"What a waste of gorgeous space," Samuel said and stepped closer.

Sully stopped him with a hand on his shoulder. "Let me go first and test things out. I'm pretty sure there is some rot or termite damage around this place." He waved the light across the porch and tested the rickety, creaky steps with his boots and weight. He made his way across the porch in the same tentative fashion. When he reached the door, he tried the latch, found it unlocked, and with a bit of force, he pushed the door in with a loud screech and grinding of wood.

"Hmm. Needs looking at," he said and moved the light around.

"What do you see?"

"Cobwebs and a shitload of dust bunnies took over along with a couple of other furry critters who needed a home. Most of the windows are broken, glass all over, and a few holes in the floor. Otherwise, it looks fixable, but I won't know for sure until I check out the foundation," Sully said and disappeared farther into the house.

"What's the layout?"

"Looks like a great room with the kitchen and stone fireplace, and off in the back I see three doors, perhaps two bedrooms and a bathroom. I'm not sure until I get farther inside."

Sully let out a soft "Whoa there!" as the floor creaked with a loud protest.

"Get your ass back out here," Dakota called out. "We don't want you to risk a limb."

"Yeah, I'm coming out," Sully said as he reappeared in the doorway. He brushed cobwebs off his shoulders and sneezed. "Whew, there's a lot of build-up."

"Bless you," Dakota said in a mild tone.

"What do you think? Can it be fixed?" Samuel asked Sully.

"I'll bring a couple of inspectors to check out this place. Depending on what they find, I'll know more about the options," Sully said.

"Why would you want to fix this place? We should tear it down," Dakota said.

Samuel glanced at Dakota. "Think about it, if this gets fixed, you can move out of the third floor and into here for privacy. We could hire an in-house manager and turn some of the third floor into a private apartment for them as part of their pay. Or we can turn this into a specialized honeymooners' suite or other separate cabin for various get-togethers."

Dakota scratched his chin. "It's an idea."

"We don't know nothing until it gets checked out," Sully said as he slammed the door closed behind him. He headed down the steps.

"Good. Get everything running across the board. You're hired, of course," Samuel said, and held out his hand.

Sully chuckled and shook hands. "Good. I'll send over a contract when I get back to the office and get things moving once it's signed."

"Perfect. Let's get out of here." Samuel looked around, figured out his bearings with a turn from Dakota, and stomped off through the grass. "This needs to be mowed."

The taller males laughed and followed him out.

* * * *

Hours later, Samuel sat back against the headboard, body sweaty and exhausted from Dakota's tender loving care. He twitched the sheet over his bare hips.

After dealing with the used condom, Dakota rolled over on his stomach and folded his arms under his head. He turned his face toward Samuel. "I'm guessing you want to talk."

"Thinking about what Sully is gonna do to this place. He's going to make her look fabulous when he's done. Isn't he?"

"Yes, but it won't be for a few months or even a year. The Charm and the little house need a lot of renovation."

"And there is more I added to the list."

"More?"

"I would like a longer boardwalk. I would adore a pergola over the band and outdoor bar area. I want a large gazebo built with a clear view of the beach and ocean."

"A pergola? A gazebo? Why?"

"Weddings. We can start to offer weddings if we had additional areas for ceremonies and guests."

"To bring in more business, but we don't have a wedding organizer or caterer. At least, I'm not quite the caterer."

"We can hire a wedding planner or find one in town or in Pensacola. First, we need to create options for the couples. I need to work out the figures and information before making any set plans."

"You're talking about long-term plans, though."

"I know. Why do you ask?"

"I thought you said you were only here for a few months for the transition to go through and on to the next site."

"In the beginning, yes, but my mother hasn't found another site. Plus, once I dove into the paperwork and saw the possibilities of making the Charm into something more than what she is, I came up with ideas. Long-term plans and ideas I want to see through."

Dakota pushed himself up until he sat facing Samuel on the bed. "How long term?"

"I want to stay as long as it takes to bring the Charm back into her prime. I also want to see what's in store for us. I don't want to leave you, Dakota."

"I didn't want you to leave either." Dakota reached out and caressed his face.

"I'm staying. Now...I have one more question."

Dakota groaned. "What is it?"

"Why are you named Dakota?"

Dakota dropped his jaw at the question.

"I can't figure it out. I wanna know."

Losing himself in laughter, Dakota dropped to the bed, arms wrapped around his waist, as he laughed.

Samuel moved to straddle his chuckling lover and poked his sides several times. "Tell me."

"Long....family...story..."

"Tell me."

"Later... I have other plans," Dakota said as he snatched Samuel down and silenced his questions with a deep, passionate kiss.

Samuel tried to break off and keep up with the questions, but Dakota tumbled them across the bed. Trapped underneath his lover, Samuel lost all reasoning. He wrapped his arms around the man's shoulders and kissed him back. At the moment, he was quite happy to stay there, in this quaint little hotel, cuddled against Dakota. There was no better option in his life.

About the Author

Ever the quiet one growing up, Nicole Dennis often slid away from reality and curled up with a book to slip into the worlds of her favorite authors. Over the years, she's created a personal library full of novels filled with dragons, fairies, vampires, shapeshifters of all kinds and romance. Always she returned to romance. Still, there were these characters in her head, worlds wanting to be built on paper, and stories wanting to be told and she began writing them down whether during or after class. She continues to this day. Only recently has it begun to become fruitful, spreading out to let others read and enter her worlds, meet her characters, and see what she sees. No matter what she writes, her stories of romance with their twists of paranormal, fantasy and erotica will always have their Happily Ever Afters.

She currently works in a quiet office in Central Florida, where she also makes her home, and enjoys the down time to slip into her characters and worlds to escape reality from time to time. At home, she becomes human slave to a semi-demonic tortie calico.

Nicole Dennis loves to hear from readers. You can find her contact information, website details and author profile page at http://www.totallybound.com.

Totally Bound Publishing